A skeletal, purplish-gray, humanoid shape hunched in the low entryway to the Silver Goblet.

Its leathery, gray skin was covered in the remnants of tattered traveling clothes so colorful they would not have looked out of place on a court jester had they not been caked with gore and mud.

In one gnarled fist it clutched what looked like a small, hairy foot. Blood ran down onto its bare chest from its open, toothy mouth. The thing's empty eye sockets flickered red as it flung its jaws wide and screeched.

**From the creators of the
greatest roleplaying game ever
come tales of heroes fighting
monsters with magic!**

By T.H. Lain

T.H. Lain

THE LIVING DEAD

Distributed in the United States by Holtzbrinck Publishing.
Distributed in Canada by Fenn Ltd.

Distributed to the hobby, toy, and comic trade in the United States and Canada by regional distributors.

Distributed worldwide by Wizards of the Coast, Inc. and regional distributors.

Cover art by Todd Lockwood
First Printing: May 2002
Library of Congress Catalog Card Number: 2001097132

9 8 7 6 5 4 3 2 1

US ISBN: 0-7869-2848-4
UK ISBN: 0-7869-2849-2
620-88230-001-EN

U.S., CANADA,
ASIA, PACIFIC, & LATIN AMERICA
Wizards of the Coast, Inc.
P.O. Box 707
Renton, WA 98057-0707
+1-800-324-6496

EUROPEAN HEADQUARTERS
Wizards of the Coast, Belgium
P.B. 2031
2600 Berchem
Belgium
+32-70-23-32-77

Visit our web site at **www.wizards.com**

Living Dead-ications

This book is dedicated to Dave,
Toby, Chris, Jesse, Shoe,
Thomasson, Will, and Cam.
Mungo live. Mungo smash.
Mungo die.

The author wishes to thank the
3rd Edition D&D® illustrators
for the creepy wights and
slinky wizards; Messrs. Gordon,
Jackson, O'Bannon, Raimi, and
Romero for all the flesh-eating
creeps; and Mrs. Lain.

Special thanks to the
supernaturally patient
Jess Lebow.

"The prophecy!" howled the little old woman. "Your coming was foretold!"

Every head in the crowded, smoky confines of the Silver Goblet tavern turned to peer at the goggled-eyed, humpbacked crone. She jabbed her index finger at a tall, young elf woman in golden robes and a man with a lute slung over one shoulder. The two swiveled in their seats, regarded the harridan with equal degrees of puzzlement, glanced at each other, then tried to concentrate on their drinks. Although the pair sat on adjacent stools at the bar, they seemed not to know one another. The elf woman sipped self-consciously from a glass of white liquid while the man guzzled his second mug of ale.

"It is you! The lute and the—the hair! The wild black hair! It is prophesied!" She let the last word end in another good screech for emphasis, but undercut herself by asking, "Or is that 'prophesized'?"

The elf woman was obviously a traveling wizard—her waist was hung with leather bags and scroll pouches, her shoulders were crisscrossed by packs laced with pockets and sleeves, and a black wand tipped with a flame-colored stone was thrust through her belt. She opened her mouth to ask if the old woman might accept a copper coin and leave, but the lutist held up his hand. He was curious to hear where this was going. The wizard, Mialee, held her tongue but could not restrain a smirk. The bard had finished a set of ballads half an hour earlier. It had been impossible not to notice him staring at Mialee while he sang. Happily, his attention diverted the moment the first mug of ale hit the table in front of him.

His stare was not that surprising, she supposed. His softly pointed ears betrayed his partial elf blood. Other than him and Mialee, there were no other elves in the place. He probably thought she'd be a pushover to his brooding musician act.

The man grinned and ran a hand through a thick head of black hair. As the shriveled creature argued with herself about word choice in public prophecy, he broke into a melodious laugh that boomed throughout the smoke-filled tavern.

Mialee sipped her milk and rolled her eyes.

"It was a message," the woman whispered. "A warning, of black days and horrors to walk the earth." She sidled up to their stools and rather rudely stuck her nose between them. The woman might have been four and a half feet tall, but she looked even shorter than that because a grotesque hump and twist in her spine forced her into a bent stance. Mialee wondered how the woman could walk without a cane to support herself. The old body was bent down as if tremendous weights were hung about her shoulders. She wriggled her backside to the bar and sat on the wooden foot rail below the counter.

The tiny woman peered up at the pair with twinkling, mischievous eyes. "You don't believe old *gakkakkgek*—"

Mialee blinked and turned back to her glass of milk. This was not the woman's name, but a sound the hag made when preparing to spit something truly monstrous onto the bar floor.

"—old me! Listen up!"

She jammed her fingers into either knee that sat a few inches from her tiny, cauliflower ears, and cackled as the pair jumped in tandem. The old woman hacked and spit once more for good measure, then launched into a singsong ditty that made no sense whatever to Mialee.

> "One and one and one is three,
> "One for the elder, one is for me,
> "The Buried walks beneath thee,
> "The Buried walks beneath thee,
> "Elf on my left, lute gold and prudent,
> "Elf on my right, black-haired student,
> "Elf yet to come, guardian true,
> "One elf is the teacher,
> "The last one is his muse.
> "Death beneath the sleeping mount
> "But wait they must for the day he counts."

Something about the way the old woman looked at Mialee made her uneasy, and it wasn't the smell, the twisted hump, or the bug-eyed stare directed somewhere above her right ear. The old woman smelled of illusion. She also had terrible grammar.

Mialee spoke the soft elvish words of a minor detection spell to take a closer look at the cackling little creature.

"What?" said the man on the stool next to hers.

Mialee faked a few coughs. "Nothing. Prophecies. Never had any use for them."

The woman raved about flame, death, and the end of the world as Mialee focused the spell. The old crone was wearing an illusion all right, it was all over her. Mialee couldn't make out what sort of creature was hidden beneath the magical energy. Whatever she was, the crone had not actually threatened anyone, but only warned them about the end of the world.

"Old woman," Mialee said, "or old man, why do you disguise your true appearance with illusion? I admire the strength of the spell. Who are you? What is your true shape?"

"Wha—er, arr! Fire, and doom, dead walk the earth! Await the one in the garish robes with the silver hair! It is foretold!" the crone babbled quickly, suddenly sounding much younger than she looked, and much less sure of herself.

The half-elf beside Mialee gaped but said nothing. Mialee heard him hum a short refrain without touching the lute, then gasp. She didn't need to look to feel the subtle, magical vibrations of his detection spell. Interesting. She knew some performers could harness arcane sorcery with harmonically sensitive energy, but she'd only met a few. Most were con men, or worse.

The crone straightened and grew by a foot as she spread her arms and backed to the door. The little woman turned and bolted out the swinging doors of the Silver Goblet Inn.

Mialee returned to her milk. The bard stared at her for a second, then tipped his ale glass.

"Can I do something for you?" Mialee asked.

The man with "lute gold and prudent"—had the little troll really said "gold and *prudent*?"—laughed. "Not right now, miss. By the way, I wouldn't recommend ordering much more of that milk. I know where Gurgitt gets it."

Mialee eyed her milk queasily and pushed it away. "Thanks."

"No problem."

The elf woman reached into a pack and removed a small, leather-bound book embossed with silver runes that stated simply "Spellbook" in Elvish and a magical quill that never needed dipping. She scribbled a few equations and notes in arcane script. Occasionally Mialee ducked her head to the bar with frequent, furtive squints at the yellowed pages. She was not keen on her bad eyesight becoming public knowledge.

Life in the cold, northern forests could be dangerous for a traveling wizard, and she'd done plenty of exploration over the past decade or two. Trickier to explore were the secrets of earning a living, which usually involved delving into some hole in the ground or setting up shop in a place like Dogmar. The knowledge she gained was worth the trouble, though. She'd learned that from old Favrid. Now she sat in this stinkhole because of him.

An old teacher of hers, Favrid had summoned her to this olfactory gauntlet of a tavern. He was a day late. And he wore garish robes. Whoever the strange little woman had really been, Mialee was not surprised she'd known the old man. Old Favrid knew a lot of people stranger than that.

The wizard woman found the entire city of Dogmar distasteful. The place simply smelled. Thousands of dwarves, half-elves, humans, halflings, and gnomes, maybe even half-orcs, were crammed together in a seemingly random jumble of wooden buildings on the edge of the only decent harbor for miles. The roads made no sense, and Mialee had gotten lost constantly over the last day and a half trying to navigate the stinking place. The odors of all these people, most of whom were in serious need of a bath, mingled with the smell of dead fish wafting in from the docks. This was smothered in the aroma of a hundred different foods coming from inn kitchens and street vendors. Under it all flowed a rich current of sewage.

If the smell was bad, the people themselves were even harder to take. Four times she'd caught someone trying to pick her pocket. Even when she threatened to turn them into toads—truthfully, an empty threat—criminals continued to plague her.

The front doors to the tavern swung inward, and Mialee cast her gaze over the smoke-filled room again, hoping to see her old teacher, the wise and ancient Favrid. The man was impossible to miss. He was almost seven feet tall, had flowing white hair to his waist, and a tendency to outrageously mismatch the colors of his silk robes.

Mialee wasn't at all surprised when the old man didn't stride through the doorway. Instead, she directed her gaze downward to see a gang of three rough-looking halflings. One strutted in an outlandishly expensive-looking suit. Behind him tagged a burly, nearly five-foot male in an undersized vest, torn pants, and a rope tied around his waist. He would call the halfling in the suit "sir" every chance he got. Bringing up the rear was a red-haired female in hand-sewn fur clothes and a fur cape. Wrapped in all that fur, Mialee half expected the fire-haired little woman to bark like a dog as she passed the far end of the bar.

The halfling dandy called out to the barkeep for a round of ales and headed to a darkened table in the rear. The redhead followed, while the halfling giant waited at the bar to carry the drinks. The Silver Goblet wasn't lavish with its waiters. In nearly two days, Mialee hadn't seen anyone working in the tavern except the bartender/owner and a few bitter, angry dwarves hauling trash and struggling to repair the soot-streaked, smoking fireplace. Every one of the dwarves looked as if he'd been rolled in ashes, and none of them were tavern employees. The whole place ran on Gurgitt, who never stepped out from behind the bar. Rumor held that there was a Mrs. Gurgitt in the kitchen, who cooked like a madwoman and liked to set rat traps. Mialee heard them snapping all night. She tried not to let her mind jump to any conclusions.

One last halfling entered, slamming the wooden slats of the swinging door back a little too conspicuously, and the bard beside her jumped a little too high. She frowned at the man beside her, lost in his third ale, then decided to frown at the halfling instead. He was a fat, bearded little fellow wearing a cloak sewn together from semi-tanned animal hides much rattier than the redheaded female's. Next to a brown eye patch, one monocular orb studied Mialee for a split second, then followed his companions into the tavern.

Another thief, Mialee concluded. This was where Favrid had to meet her? Why in the name of holy Elohnna did it have to be in this lawless hellhole? Why did that halfling stare at her just now?

Mialee had been stared at plenty of times in her hundred years, but something about the halfling's gaze made her check for her purse. The small, leather bag hung safely from her belt. Mialee had been traveling for years since she struck out on her own, but generally tried to avoid cities if she could help it. She'd take open tundra over a place like Dogmar.

Favrid actually loved places like this. During her apprenticeship to the old elf, he'd consistently found ways to arrange their lodging in the most crowded and malodorous section of the biggest city around. Lacking a city, he'd make do with a large town that thought it was a city, as was the case here. Favrid claimed to revel in the diversity of experiences and people. The old man insisted it taught him far more than any book he'd read or any lecture he'd witnessed.

But Mialee also knew the old man's sense of humor. He knew she hated staying in cities. He was probably just trying to teach her a lesson about humility, or observation, or odor control.

So she waited.

Mialee hadn't drunk anything stronger than milk in decades. She'd tried wine a few times in her youth, and the result had always been headaches and general disaster. Some elves had the constitution to consume alcohol as freely as humans, more were completely immune to its intoxicating effects. A few, like Mialee, had an almost allergic reaction to liquor that greatly enhanced the effect of intoxication, but also accelerated it through her metabolism at dizzying speed. In short, when Mialee drank, she became twice as drunk in half the time and finished the experience with ten times the hangover. Her mother told her to enjoy it, at least while Mialee was young. It ran in the family, evidence of "royal blood" or some similar nonsense.

Mialee respected her mother, but sometimes wondered if the woman was insane. Waiting for her old teacher to show up in the chaotic, smoky tavern, she speculated that insanity might be something that happened to every elf in old age. Elders probably kept it from anyone under five hundred.

Maybe her old mentor had been trying to teach her a lesson by meeting in the tavern under the Silver Goblet sign. Or maybe Favrid had simply forgotten their appointment—*he* was over a thousand years old. Mialee sighed and stared at the door, willing Favrid to walk through.

The doors remained still. Mialee waved to the barkeep, who was busy pouring golden liquid into a fluted glass. The hulking man nodded and waddled over to her with the glass still in his hand.

"Gurgitt, do you have any water that I could actually see daylight through?" asked the elf woman.

A wide smile cracked the man's thick, black beard, and he set the fluted glass on the bar in front of her. "I can do better than that, mistress elf," the barkeep rumbled conspiratorially. "This here is from the gentleman." He jammed a finger in the musician's face and added, "and it's coming out of your pay."

Mialee recognized when someone was paying too much attention to her. She supposed that all those years staying in cities with Favrid had taught her something, after all. She pushed the glass back to the barkeep.

"Save it for someone who will appreciate the vintage. Maybe a cup of tea?"

The barkeep shrugged, nodded, produced a funnel from somewhere beneath the counter, and waddled off to return the liquid to its bottle.

The bard shifted to look at her, and Mialee readied herself to disappoint him. She had hours of study remaining tonight if she was going to finish her spellwork.

"Ow!" Her barstool squealed as the half-elf's hand moved behind her with surprising speed.

Mialee whirled in her seat, very nearly falling to the floor. To her surprise, the bard's hand steadied her before she went over. She shrugged off his grip.

The bard held a halfling ear in his other hand. The ear was attached to the halfling with the eyepatch. Mialee noted with mild disgust that the patch looked like the dried ear of some large canine. The little man clutched something tightly to his breast. Something, Mialee noted, with two familiar leather straps.

"Ow! Devis, what are you—OW! Ow, ow, ow, ow!" the halfling cried. The little scoundrel had nicked her pouch of spell components. She arched an eyebrow at the smelly, pint-sized thief.

The halfling snarled and recovered some grasp of his vocabulary.

"Devis, what the hell!" he boomed in a surprisingly deep voice.

The bard simply stared at the little man, and Mialee actually saw him make a slight, rolling 'get on with it' motion with his finger. He was scheming all right. The halfling and half-elf were blatantly in cahoots.

"She's just begging to be robbed. Look at her!"

"I am," the bard replied, "and I don't think she's very happy with you right now, Hound-Eye. You see," he said through clenched teeth, "my new friend . . ." (he twisted the halfling's ear at the word "friend") ". . . and I just happen to be named together in a prophecy. Big, local legend. She and I, and some schoolteacher. And maybe we should just be left alone."

The bard waggled his eyebrows. If they weren't targeting her, the pair's incompetence might have been funny, but now they simply irritated Mialee.

The bard, still clutching the halfling's ear and Mialee's shoulder, turned to the elf woman.

"Miss, meet Hound-Eye, the sharpest pickpocket in Dogmar. Or at least the sharpest one in the Silver Goblet," he added, casting a look around.

"That's my sp—" Mialee caught herself before she revealed the pouch's true nature. She'd learned long ago the danger of casually revealing the source of one's power, and she'd nearly blurted the secret. "—my pouch full of birdseed. Birdseed," she finished lamely. "I have this bird, and . . . Look, I study magic, and prophecies are a load of —"

"Hound-Eye, I believe you have something belonging to the lady," the bard said, twisting the halfling's ear a bit. Hound-Eye let out a yelp and dropped the familiar leather pouch to the tavern floor. The thief kicked the bard hard in the shin, wriggled from the half-elf's grasp, and scrambled out the swinging doors.

The bard watched the thief leave and reached down to rub his shin. He hooked the pouch with one finger and tossed it up over his shoulder to Mialee, who snatched it from the air. "Your birdseed?" the bard grunted, then straightened.

Mialee tied the pouch into place at her waist, tucking it safely under her wide, leather belt. "Thank you . . . Devis, is it?"

"The one and only," the bard said, bowing with just a little too much flourish. "And please, don't mention it. We don't see many elves around here. Perhaps in return for my good deed," he continued, settling into the empty stool next to hers as he signaled Gurgitt with a wave of his hand, "You might join me for a glass?" The barkeep caught the movement and waddled to comply.

"No, thank you, really." Mialee reached instinctively for her purse. "I have no head for wine or ale. Let me give you something." She fumbled for a silver piece. Devis leaned onto the bar, turned to the elf woman, and held up a palm.

"Please, you wound me," he said, "I'm not looking for money. Just a few minutes with the most beautiful girl in Dogmar."

Was he serious?

"May I ask your name?" Devis pressed. He flashed her a lopsided smile she suspected was meant to be utterly disarming. Despite her irritation, she had to admit he was on to something there.

"Mialee," she replied in surrender as Gurgitt arrived with a small pot of minty-smelling tea and a foamy brown ale. He placed the former before the bard, the latter in front of Mialee, then lumbered back to his work.

"I wouldn't think of forcing liquor on someone with no taste for it," said Devis, nimbly swapping the drinks. "Don't see many elves around here," the bard said over a gulp of ale.

"I'm not surprised," she said, pouring tea into a small, ceramic cup. The elf woman glanced at the man's ears and added, "How do you stand the smell?"

"You get used to it," he laughed. "Besides, mother was human."

"Lucky," Mialee said. "Mine was a lunatic."

She resigned herself to the conversation and sipped at the tea. To her surprise, it was quite good. Mialee grinned despite the unpleasant atmosphere. She had a weakness for musicians.

"Mialee, you'll pardon me for saying so, but you don't fit in here."

"You're right, Devis," said Mialee, "I'm not looking to. I'm here to meet a friend."

Devis took another slug of his ale. "I can help. I know this town pretty well, maybe I can help you find your friend."

"I doubt it," Mialee replied. "He's not from around here, either. In fact, I have absolutely no idea why he wanted to meet me here."

Mialee, have you found Favrid? A voice reverberated in her temple.

"No, Biksel, I haven't, and I'm busy being prophetically wooed," she blurted to the air. Normally, she would have communicated silently with her familiar, but the raven's sudden, mental intrusion caught her off guard.

"Pardon?" Devis asked.

"Nothing," said Mialee.

You locked me in the bloody wardrobe, Mialee, the voice reverberated in her head. *It smells, and there's nothing to eat. And I can see what you're doing.*

So what? You can always see what I'm doing. I've gotten over it. You're locked in for your own safety, Biksel.

Mialee had had it. She flashed a mental image to him of the previous night, when the little raven had very nearly been hacked to pieces by the innkeeper's wife after trying to make off with some food from the kitchen.

If you're really hungry, I can have Mrs. Gurgitt bring something up, she added as she swallowed a mouthful of tea.

No, that's all right, Biksel replied, and Mialee could have sworn she heard him sigh. *But I'll be keeping an eye on you.*

Fine, Mialee told her familiar. She saw the bard looking at her quizzically. *Just keep quiet for a while, could you? I might have someone here who can help us find Favrid.*

Is that a musician?

Shut up, Biksel.

Her familiar did not reply, which Mialee took as compliance with her request. Sometimes, you just had to know how to think at the bird.

Still, she knew Biksel would be using their connection to keep tabs on this conversation. He was getting impatient.

"All right," Mialee said, "Maybe you can do something for me." She swiveled in conspiratorially. "I'm looking for a thousand year-old elf named Favrid. About five and a half feet tall, mostly bald. Talks to himself a lot. Terrible short-term memory. Likes garish robes. Probably has a raven on his shoulder."

Devis bit his lip in a show of concentration, but Mialee could see he didn't recognize the name.

"Sorry," he explained, "doesn't ring a bell. Do you think your friend might be in trouble?"

"I don't know what to think," Mialee said, and frustration overcame the pleasant effect of the tea. "It's ridiculous! I received a message to meet him at this tavern. And it had to be this week."

"Is he a scholar?" asked Devis.

"A wizard like me," Mialee replied, the calming tea and charming bard making her abandon her usual reticence. "He was one of my teachers. But I haven't seen him for ten years. Last I'd heard he was researching some tomb he discovered in the southern desert."

"Maybe he was simply delayed," Devis suggested.

"He was only specific about one thing—the date I was to meet him here," Mialee said, shaking her head. She took another sip of tea. "That part seemed important."

"So what will you do now?" the bard asked.

"Keep waiting. I guess I can give him another day, then I'll begin looking for him." Mialee assessed the bard. "You know, you might be some help there, too. If I have to find Favrid . . . there's a name he mentioned. I don't know whether it's a person or a place."

"You don't know where to start looking," Devis said. "I would be honored to help."

"I am certain you will be," Mialee said. "There were two names, actually. They sounded familiar, but I can't seem to find anyone who wants to talk to me about them. The words seem to spook a lot of people."

"Morkeryth?"

"It's Mork—" Mialee blinked. "How did you know that?"

"It's a ruin, not far from here. Maybe a couple of days' foot travel on the road, then a day or so to get through the forest of Silath. I know a few trails," Devis said.

"Silath? The other place was called "Silatham.""

"Silatham!" the bard exclaimed. "Heard of it, but it's a myth. Ancient elf village, supposed to be loaded with treasure and weapons. Every few weeks someone comes into Tent City—that's a halfling camp on the Morkeryth ruins—and announces they're going to find, or have just found, Silatham, 'lost outpost of the elves'."

"What are you, some kind of ranger?" Mialee asked.

"No, just a wandering bard with a half-empty ale glass, I'm afraid." He signaled Gurgitt for another round. Mialee refused more of the tea.

"So, tell me about this ruin."

Devis slapped a coin on the table and took a swallow from his refilled glass. "It's a ruin, but it's not uninhabited. Morkeryth spooks most people here in Dogmar, but that makes it a good place for people to—well, hide."

"What kind of people?" Mialee asked.

"People who don't want to be found," the bard explained unhelpfully.

The elf woman opened her mouth to ask another question as the wooden door slammed inward with a loud crack.

A skeletal, purplish-gray, humanoid shape hunched in the low entryway to the Silver Goblet. Its leathery, gray skin was covered in the remnants of tattered traveling clothes so colorful they would not have looked out of place on a court jester had they not been caked with gore and mud. In one gnarled fist it clutched what looked like a small, hairy foot. Blood ran down onto its bare chest from its open, toothy mouth. The thing's empty eye sockets flickered red as it flung its jaws wide and screeched. Lightning flashed, casting the skeletal figure in silhouette.

"And those kind, I'm afraid," Devis said softly over Mialee's shoulder.

A cacophony erupted from every corner of the tavern. Mialee had to grip the bar to keep her balance as the current of sweaty, bellowing bodies trampled toward the back of the room, apparently hoping to escape through the kitchen whether Mrs. Gurgitt liked it or not. Heavy thumps told her Gurgitt was lumbering kitchenward at top speed to explain the situation to his wife personally.

The fingers of Mialee's right hand twirled in a short, complicated gesture, and she whispered a few words in Elvish. She raised her glowing fingertips to blast the monster with golden energy. At last, something interesting was happening.

Unaware or uncaring of what Mialee was doing, Devis drew a long sword and leaped between her and the skeletal thing in the door. In passing, the bard knocked her hand aside. The golden fire sputtered and died on her fingers.

Angrily she shouted at her would-be savior. Devis foolishly risked a glance back at the wizard.

The screeching thing's eyes flashed as it saw the opening. It leaped into the now-deserted tavern with animal speed and caught the bard across the jaw with one bone-knuckled fist. Devis flew backward and flopped onto the bar amid the clutter of glasses, cups, and half-eaten dinners littering the countertop.

"Idiot," Mialee repeated, but hoped the bard was all right. She concentrated on retrieving her aborted spell. Her fingers brushed a tiny pearl in one pocket of her robe and she felt the power surge anew.

The gray creature swiveled its wire-haired skull on a ropy neck. It hissed in wordless challenge.

Mialee's hand finished shaping the spell, and she chopped the air in front of her face. A ball of golden fire erupted from her splayed digits and drove at the speed of magic into the thing's torso.

The monster staggered back, smoke curling up from its charred clothing and blackened skin. The back of its skull struck the low archway and it stopped with a snarl.

Mialee heard the clink of glasses and saw Devis roll off of the bar and land next to her in a crouch. He fumbled on the floor and retrieved his sword. Mialee searched her mind for another useful spell. She hadn't expected to go into combat today, so most of the spells she'd memorized were aids to her studies—detection spells, light spells, and divinations. Was there nothing else?

Well, she always had her wand of missiles. Failing that, a rapier hung from her waist, smacking against her leg. But first she slipped the polished wooden wand into her hand and prepared to meet the creature's attack.

The assault came, but not from the skeletal shape smoldering in the doorway. A ball of brown and white fur slammed into the intruder from behind, knocking the blood-caked thing face-first to the floor. Hound-Eye straddled the lanky monster and raised a heavy mining pick over his head. With a high-pitched yell of anguish and fury, the halfling plunged the pick into the back of the creature's skull. Twice. Three times. Black gore, bits of yellowed bone sprouting wiry hair, and leathery chunks of flesh spattered into the air.

After a half-minute, the creature finally stopped squirming around the pick that staked its head to the floor. Its skull was a ruin, its neck torn and broken. A viscous puddle bloomed around the whole affair and spread over the floorboards.

Hound-Eye rolled off the creature and moaned at the ceiling. He clutched gingerly at a makeshift, sodden, red bandage covering the stump of his left ankle. Mialee looked at the dead thing's knotted fist, still clutching the hairy little foot, and realized with sickening certainty where the creature had found its lucky charm.

"Hound-Eye!" Devis shouted. He dropped his sword and ran to the agonized halfling. "Mialee, Gurgitt always keeps a stock of potions behind the bar," he called over his shoulder.

Mialee blinked and hesitated, then swept glasses from the countertop and clambered over to the bar. Her sharp eyes scanned the open shelves, looking for vials of healing magic. She saw several unlabeled wooden boxes that could have held anything from blasting powder to gnomish beer, for all she could tell.

Hound-Eye screamed pitiably. Devis shouted, "Hurry, Mialee, he's going into shock!"

"Where are they?" said Mialee.

"I don't know, behind the bar!" Devis yelled, panic creeping into his voice. "In a wooden box, I think." More quietly, the bard said, "Look at me, Hound-Eye. Focus on my eyes, little guy. Come on. How many fingers am I holding up?"

"Blue," mumbled the halfling.

Mialee flung several unlabeled crates from the shelves, shattering bottles of liquor and clay pots full of dried meat onto the floor with no sign of any medicine. Then her eyes fell on a stack of laundered towels. They would have to do. She grabbed the top few and an unbroken bottle of dark green liquid with Orcish script on the label. That had to be potent, she guessed.

Magic, Mialee had found in her studies, was sometimes not the only solution to a problem. The wizard often traveled alone in dangerous country, and had gotten used to rationing any healing magic tightly and to treat minor injuries with non-magical methods whenever she could. Favrid had drummed the practice into her during their travels, and she'd never lost the basic skills.

The elf woman sprang to the bartop and rolled over it sideways, bounced onto her booted feet, and stepped into the goo surrounding the remains of the gray monster's head. Her feet flew forward beneath her and she slammed backward into the bar, then the floor. She stared up at the tobacco-stained ceiling of the Silver Goblet tavern through a red wash of pain. The orc liquor bottle seemed suspended in midair, slowly tumbling end over end above her. Bar towels fluttered down like wet leaves.

A fingerless glove flashed into her vision and deftly clasped the neck of the spinning bottle inches above her temple.

"Thanks," Devis said.

Mialee winced. "Don't—*ow*—mention it. Couldn't find the potions."

"Yeah, I guessed. This works for now," Devis said, examining the Orcish label. "Drek grog. Good year." The bard twisted the cork into his fingers and took a long draw from the bottle. He grimaced and gasped, eyes bulging. "Smooth," he croaked.

Mialee crawled on all floors and collected the bar towels, leaving those that had landed in monster-gore. She handed them to Devis, who upended the bottle of clear liquor and emptied half of the contents onto the handful of rags.

"Hound-Eye, I've got to clean this, or you're going to die," Devis said loudly into the moaning halfling's one-eyed face.

"Gonna," the halfling huffed, "kill you."

"I know, pal," said Devis. "Sit up. This'll help."

Mialee supported the halfling's head as the bard poured clear liquor across Hound-Eye's paling lips. The halfling swallowed weakly.

"Better," he croaked. "Still gonna kill you."

"Later, Hound-Eye. Mialee, take one of these rags and stuff it in his mouth."

"What?" the elf woman asked incredulously.

"He needs something to bite on," the bard explained. "This is going to sting a little." Without another word, Devis jerked Hound-Eye's blood-soaked bandage from the stump.

Mialee's ears rang as the halfling screamed through the alcohol-soaked rag stuffed between his lips. Blood oozed from the meaty end of the ankle around a jagged sliver of bone.

"Hound-Eye, get ready!" Devis shouted. He upended the liquor bottle over Hound-Eye's ankle and emptied it over the torn flesh and shattered bone.

Mialee nodded as the bard gently packed the liquor-soaked bar rags around Hound-Eye's wound. She hoped Devis knew what he was doing. The halfling's screams would deafen her soon.

A voice invaded her thoughts. *Can't a bird get a minute of sleep around here? What—?* The rest of the message was an incomprehensible sensation of confusion in Mialee's brain.

Not now, Biksel. I'm fine.

The halfling went limp and drew steady, wheezing breaths around the rag between his teeth.

"Mialee, hold this."

Devis indicated the rags bunched around the stump, and Mialee rested the halfling's head and shifted her hands to the bandages. Tiny red dots showed on the white towels where blood was already soaking through, but red was better than green, Mialee guessed. Devis produced a length of silk rope from a coil on his belt and wound it tightly several times around the entire bundle. He produced a jackknife from somewhere and cut the rope from the coil at his belt. His fingers flew as he tied the tourniquet off with a complicated knot, then sat back, breathing hard.

Mialee heard heavy footsteps thumping the floorboards. Gurgitt was back. Mialee heard the man emit a low groan as he took in the damage.

"Gurgitt," she called as she climbed to her feet, careful not to slip in ghoul innards. "I'll take that wine now."

"That old man had better show up soon. You know—" Mialee waved a wobbly index finger in Devis' face—"I'm going to kill him."

Mialee slumped over her wine glass. Two empty bottles of Gurgitt's finest sat on the bar before her, next to four or five empty ale glasses. Devis was having trouble keeping track.

The elf woman had claimed to have no head for wine, but the girl could *drink*.

"Kill. Him. If he's not dead," she added with the glass-eyed emphasis of the truly holy or the truly drunk.

Devis nodded dimly at her oath, but his eyes were on Gurgitt. The barkeeper was pushing his considerable bulk through the crowd gathered around the fallen ghoul, clutching a smelly stable blanket in one hand and a meat cleaver in the other.

The crowd stood back as Gurgitt grunted and snarled his way through the necessary deed of dismembering the creature. Though its head was all but gone, most people in Dogmar would never bury an intact ghoul corpse for fear of having to deal with it again.

Hound-Eye would survive, thanks to the bard and the wizard.

Devis was relieved. He'd never intended to get the little guy muti-lated with his scheme. Not that Devis expected the halfling to run headfirst into a ghoul when he left the tavern. When the bard slipped him a gold piece to filch the wizard girl's purse—so that he, Devis, could stop the crime, of course—he had every intention of buying Hound-Eye an ale or two to make up for it. They'd always gotten along well, and had helped each other out of tight spots.

The burly barkeep knelt and rolled the ruined creature's limbs and carcass onto the canvas with a look of disgust. Someone from the crowd told the big man not to let his wife get hold of the pieces, and Gurgitt stood abruptly, the messy bundle over one shoulder.

"I know where everything is, and how much money's in the cashbox, y'bastards," he growled to the assembly. "Devis will tell me if any of you try anything."

With that, the big man marched out into the rainy night through the ruined entrance to his tavern. Every pair of eyes in the Silver Goblet fell on Devis, including Mialee's.

"You a security guard, now, Devvy-Boy?" a black-bearded gnome squeaked from the crowd. The gnome's hand strayed to the hilt of a long knife.

Devis gulped. He heard Mialee snigger.

"You look like you could use some air," Devis said, turning to her so quickly he nearly lost his balance and fell from his stool. "Would you like to go for a walk?"

Without waiting for her to reply, he slid to the floor and offered her his arm. He wobbled unsteadily and flashed a lopsided grin that no woman could resist—he hoped.

"Devish," Mialee smiled, "I'd love to."

Devis thought he heard a voice shout "You're drunk!" in his mind, but decided he must be imagining it. After all, he *was* drunk.

The rest of their walk took them as far as the steps leading up to Mialee's room.

Well, that took long enough, Biksel announced inside Mialee's head as the bard snored softly next to the elf woman.

Go to blazes, Biksel.

Mialee couldn't sleep.

Literally. Elves did not sleep. Her people had no physical need for an unconscious state that stole a third of one's waking life. An elf could tire, but they banished simple fatigue with meditation and inactivity.

Mialee desperately wished she could sleep. Her head pounded, the painful reminder of earlier excesses. Devis had no such trouble. Mialee felt his warm body next to hers and listened as the bard snored softly. He slept, of course. He had human blood. She hated him for his infuriatingly satisfied dozing.

A loud crash erupted from the foot of the bed as the door was flung open.

Mialee blinked and leaned up to see what fresh hell had entered her life now.

She had to be hallucinating. A trio of dwarves stood in the doorway. The biggest one held a heavy axe over one shoulder and wore a blue leather sash that looked like a badge of official position.

"Devis! Looks like you picked the wrong place to hide out tonight."

That was a real dwarf, all right, no hallucination. Beside her, Mialee felt Devis struggle to rise to a standing position on the bed. He failed, but was wildly successful at tangling himself in the sheets and rolling headfirst off the mattress and onto the floor, taking all of the blankets with him. Mialee had more luck without the burden of covers, and rose naked on wobbly knees and uneven mattress to face the dwarves. She strove to calm her mind and think of some spell that could get her out of this ridiculous situation.

"Muhn, I was just about to come see you," Devis said from the floor. He finally freed himself from the bedclothes and stood. He wasn't wearing anything either. "You wouldn't happen to be holding a private card game tonight, would you?"

The dwarf cackled, and the other two joined in the laughter. "You've fleeced me too many times, bard. No more games. I'd take the shirt off your back, but under the circumstances, I'll settle for you."

Mialee saw the two dwarves who had not yet spoken advance on either side, their axes raised menacingly. The blue-sashed dwarf veered to intercept Devis, axe clutched in both gauntleted hands.

Mialee didn't wait for their next move. She was loath to use the last of her magic, but could see no alternative.

"GET OUT OF MY ROOM!"

She shot her index finger forward at the nearest dwarf, moving toward her right side. The dwarf stopped leering at her and followed the faint, blue line that shot from Mialee's fingertip straight into the center of the dwarf's breastplate. Crackling ice crystals formed instantly around the spot and grew outward. In moments the man's wiry beard was frozen to the metal on his chest. The dwarf squirmed and danced in a flailing panic as the ice spread and the temperature plunged inside his armor plate.

Ray of frost, Mialee heard Biksel's voice echo in her temple. *Well done, Mialee. But don't catch a chill yourself. Can I offer you a feather?*

Choke on a worm, Biksel.

The dwarf gave up trying to wriggle free of his frigid armor and ran screaming from the room.

The ray was her last offensive spell. She could cast no more until she could study her book again, but she was willing to bet the remaining dwarves didn't know that. She whispered a cantrip, a minor effect that could cause no real harm, and glared as illusory fire engulfed her hand.

"Ice and fire, spirits of darkness, I command you to engulf

THE LIVING DEAD

these foolish dwarves in the flame of vengeance!" she bellowed in her mightiest voice of doom.

No elf wizard ever spoke the common language when invoking a spell, but Mialee was willing to bet the dwarves didn't know that, either.

The two dwarves froze as stiff as their companion's armor, jaws dropped in shock. Devis, still standing beside the bed, turned to her and smiled.

"Thanks."

"Didn't you hear me?" Mialee roared. "Get out!"

Devis pointed, openmouthed, at his own chest, obviously disbelieving that she wanted him gone.

"Yes, you! You, them, everybody! Out!"

"Very well," Devis said, "Maybe I'll see you around."

He winked, grabbed his battered lute from the bedside, jerked open the shutters and leaped, wearing only the instrument on his back, out the window into the driving rain. The bard yelped as his shoulder collided with the window frame, then he was gone.

The dwarf Devis called Muhn turned to his remaining companion and said, "Don't just stand there, idiot, circle around and find him. He can't stay on the damned roofs all night!"

The dwarf scrambled to comply, dashing out the door after his scorched comrade.

Muhn turned to the naked elf and grinned. Mialee simply raised her hand again and let a small crackle of illusory energy spark from her fingertips.

"Out," she said.

The dwarf raised his axe and continued forward. "The bard's magic whore doesn't get out of this one," he growled. "I don't know where he found you, but I'm going to find out."

Mialee's hand glowed more brightly, and she arched a single eyebrow in a gesture that carried volumes of quiet menace—she hoped. Muhn paused and his eyes flicked uncertainly to the door, then back to the elf girl.

The standoff was interrupted by a shout from outside the window. It was Muhn's lackey.

"We got 'im! He's heading out over the rooftops!"

The dwarf began backing out of the room, keeping both eyes on Mialee's glowing hand.

"I'll get out," Muhn growled, "but you just made yourself an enemy of the constable of Dogmar."

He turned on his heel and marched out the door after his quarry. Mialee closed and locked the door after him, then climbed back onto the bed to look out the window. About ten feet down was another, lower rooftop, and from her vantage point, she could see out over most of the town. Devis was gone.

Mialee collapsed onto the bed and closed her eyes again, trying to force herself to meditate. Her throbbing head refused to comply.

She heard a flap of wings as Biksel flew overhead to light upon the open windowsill.

Have you ever thought that perhaps this fascination with musicians is a bit unhealthy?

"Ow," Mialee replied. "Get me a bicarbonate of soda or you can go out the window, too."

But I don't have the—

"Shut up, Biksel."

Devis shivered as rain pounded his bare back. The cover of night should at least help hide him. A man wearing nothing but a lute on his back would have attracted attention in the daytime. If he kept to the alleys and shadows, however, he could stay hidden long enough to grab something to wear from a clothesline or rubbish heap and stave off hypothermia. If he had to, he'd grab a burlap sack and rip a hole in the top for his head.

He patted the lute slung over his shoulder. At least he'd been able to grab the instrument before he'd made his hasty exit.

After leaping from the window, he'd been able to run only a few blocks from the Silver Goblet before the adjoining rooftops gave out. Forced to ground, Devis chose this darkened walkway as the best place to avoid Constable Muhn and find something to wear. His naked, rain-soaked body was chilled to the bone.

Devis scanned the piles of detritus and trash littering the narrow cobblestone causeway but found nothing he might use to clothe himself. He checked the few doors that opened into the alley. All were locked.

He glanced back down the alley toward the street. A familiar, stout silhouette stood between Devis and the main road. Then another, and another. A clank of heavy armor and the thump of booted feet boomed down the alley toward him, lead by Muhn.

"Hey, Muhn, you're not going to believe this," Devis said, "but did you know that my, uh, my . . ." He looked around for a weapon, stalling. "My coming has been foretold! I, ah, got named in a prophecy yesterday! Yeah, if something happens to me, the evil one will gain dominion."

Muhn blinked. "What?"

Devis unslung the lute and jammed a finger at the dwarf. "Kill me and Fate herself will strike you down!" He underscored that last bit, striking a single, ominous chord on the instrument.

Muhn ripped the lute from Devis's hands and ground it beneath his boot before turning on the bard. Devis kept his hands crossed in front of his waist as the three dwarves knocked him to the wet pavement. It wasn't just the lute he was concerned about.

Fortunately, the alley was narrow. Only three of them could kick him at a time.

Mialee's eyes were still closed. Her head pounded. Her stomach was in knots. She was one hundred percent sure that she was about to die, and she cursed her weakness for musicians.

Mialee, please.

The wizard forced her eyes to open, bringing fresh agony to her skull. The sky was growing slightly brighter in the west, although the rain continued unabated. Mialee couldn't guess how long it had been since Devis made his escape, but she felt like she'd been lying there for hours.

She pushed herself to the side of the bed and onto her feet. Her legs gave her roughly a second of good, solid support before giving out. She crumpled to the floor, clutching her head. The image of the screeching, gray monstrosity from the night before flashed behind her eyelids, and her stomach twisted.

Just a minute, Biksel.

With great effort, she stood next to the bed and wobbled to the window. With a weak tug, she pulled open the shutters.

"Thank you," the bird said, then flew out to find some breakfast.

"Go choke on a grub, Biksel," Mialee replied as she dragged herself back to the bed. The bard's clothing, along with a few traveling packs, lay mingled with her own robes and equipment. She tripped over the pile and heard the jingle of coins. "Dwarves wanted that, you ass," she said to the absent Devis. "Why dincha just . . ." but the effort of speaking brought more pain, so she cursed the bard silently instead.

She pulled herself up to a sitting position and stared at the rain gusting in through the open window. The wind and cold water helped clear her head, and she swung her legs off the bed and stumbled back to the window. She marveled at the accomplishment.

The wind was refreshing, but was quickly chilling the room. She closed one shutter and reached for the other. Biksel would let her know when he needed back in.

A tiny ball of black feathers careened into her forehead beak-first. Mialee fell flat on her back. She stared at the ceiling—spinning once more, just like old times—and felt blood well up from the new gash in the center of her temple.

Mialee's right hand balled into a fist. She was going to do the unthinkable. She was going to kill her familiar and sort out the consequences later. Why had Biksel attacked her?

I didn't. What are you talking about?

"Mialee," the shape squawked in a raspy, feminine bird-voice.

Mialee reached down and cupped the tiny, battered, avian body and lifted it to eye level. The elf woman blinked blood away from her eyes.

"Mialee," the bird repeated. "Help."

The raven, who probably weighed only a third as much as Biksel soaking wet, began shuddering uncontrollably.

"Hold on," she said with soft urgency.

With one foot, she kicked at the pile of clothing and gear. Her wand with the red tip clattered to the floor, one of Mialee's extra pieces of traveling security. Her spell components, she noticed gratefully, hadn't been disturbed. Still holding the bird in two hands, she kicked again at the pile, scattering a fan of gold pieces across the floor.

Valuable as the gold was, it wasn't what Mialee was looking for. She scattered clothing, packs, some rations, her rapier, and a long sword—had Devis been wearing a long sword?—across the wooden floorboards.

Healing potions weren't there. She never traveled without a few.

Hound-Eye. She had no idea how long he'd been lurking under her stool before Devis nabbed him. She still suspected Devis of fixing that little encounter.

A pitiful warble escaped from the bird in Mialee's hands. She had to do something or she'd never find out how the creature knew her name. She had a sick feeling she already knew. She had not chosen a raven to be her familiar by accident.

Catch up with me, Biksel. My potions were stolen. I'm taking her to that temple we passed on the way in, if I can find it.

Her?

Mialee raced down the stairs, leaped over the last few and skidded into the dark and mostly empty tavern. Gurgitt stood behind the bar wiping a glass.

"Morning, mistress elf," the barkeep said cheerfully.

"Don't you ever sleep, Gurgitt?" Mialee asked.

"Oh, now and then," the fat man chuckled. "Can I be getting you something? Bandage? Towel?"

"Which way to the nearest cleric? I passed a temple on the way, but the streets are so crooked."

"That'd be the Temple of the Protector, I imagine. It's an elf temple, too." Mialee's eyes and the blood running down her face told Gurgitt she wasn't in the mood for a travelogue, and he cleared his throat. "Anyway, you came in from the north, yes? You walked right past it. Head right out the door, there, and go north up the street, take a right, two soft lefts, another right, curve around the hangin' tree to about three o'clock and head straight past Cam's All Night Clothier's. Temple's got a big silver crescent on top."

"Right," Mialee said, utterly confused but hopeful that Biksel could find the place. They'd both seen the out-of-place structure, and the raven was not confined to these malodorous streets.

"Mistress elf?" Gurgitt called as she neared the doors.

"Yes?"

"Might I recommend Cam's Clothier's? Always open," the barkeep said. "He's my cousin's sister's boy."

Mialee glanced down and noticed for the first time that she was still stark naked. A small warble came from the injured raven in her hands.

"No time," she called over her shoulder.

She kicked the swinging doors open and stepped out onto the boardwalk that lined the muddy street. Mialee considered clothing purely utilitarian, anyway. The wild bears common in the northern forests didn't care about how nattily their victims were attired, but if their victim had a pocket with a knife in it, they might take notice.

Of course, Mialee thought as her teeth began chattering, it's early autumn and it's raining. Staying warm was a perfectly acceptable utilitarian purpose.

Are you trying to freeze to death?

"N-n-no," the woman stuttered as she ran, hoping the exertion would warm her. The few citizens of Dogmar awake at this hour gaped as the shivering elf passed.

I shall fly ahead and let them know you're coming.

"D-d-do that," Mialee said.

Devis had been in the Dogmar lock-up for five hours. As the sun rose behind rainclouds, a little dim light filtered into his solitary cell. Unfortunately, the barred hole also let in a lot of moisture. Devis couldn't remember the last time he'd felt so slimy.

The only other things in the cell were a foul waste bucket that apparently had never been emptied and a few wooden bowls crusted with the remains of some gray dwarf-gruel. He himself had not been fed, but he doubted the food would be worth eating anyway.

The bard finished humming a small healing tune. He was no cleric, but his music could patch up the average dwarf-pummeling. As his wounds closed, he tried to remember a musical spell Gunnivan had sworn would shatter any stone. Something about "sound and silence, stillness in the stone . . ." That was it. He switched to Gunnivan's old tune, the lyrics coming back naturally.

The locking mechanism on the door and the black bars on his open window were carved from a hard, igneous rock the locals called deknae. Dwarves mined it from the ancient lava tubes on the north side of Morsilath—the volcano had long been extinct. Deknae became as solid as steel when treated with the right amount of heat.

A stone was a stone. Devis sang softly and imagined shattering deknae.

"Shaddup!" a deep voice boomed from one of the other cells. The voice belonged to an unseen half-orc. A cacophony of other voices shouted out support for either Devis's song or the silence of the jailhouse.

Devis continued his tune, blocking out the little arguments and petty exchanges that flew back and forth across the cells between the pro-music and anti-music factions. He didn't really expect the spell to open the lock on his first try, but he made the attempt anyway.

The arguments and chatter ceased abruptly as the door to the dungeon squealed open above them. Devis lowered his song to a subvocalization, keeping the energy of the magic going but without giving away what he was doing to the guards he heard stumbling down the stone steps. From the sound of the approaching guards, Devis could tell they were carrying a third person—a person not moving under his own power, if the sound of two dragged feet thumping against the steps was any indication. Devis held the magic ready.

The guards stopped, to Devis's surprise, right outside his cell. The stocky dwarves had an elf propped up between them, and the slender figure's bare, blond hair hung in his face as the man's head lolled over to one side. The style of his battered leather armor looked positively antique and bore savage gouges that looked to the bard like claw marks from a very large dog, or maybe a wolf. The leather armor was spattered with dark swaths—probably blood—and the pair of scabbards hitched to the elf's weapon belt hung empty. One of the elf's guards left the unconscious man with his partner, then stepped forward to unlock the barred door.

Devis let his song rise in volume, feeling a familiar, invisible aura of magical energy. He had to time the release of the spell perfectly. If he failed, he would get another beating, but if he succeeded, he might get out of this pit. The lead guard fumbled with the keys. The elf prisoner lolled back over to one side as the dwarf holding him struggled to balance the taller man's weight. Devis saw immediately that he had been wrong about the armored elf.

He wasn't unconscious at all. The elf briefly made eye contact with the bard.

The dwarf with the keys dropped the entire ring on the floor and cursed. As the guard stooped to pick them up, Devis shot a look at the "unconscious prisoner" in an effort to let him know that if he meant to try anything, now would be the time.

Devis sang, loud and clear. He heard the deknae lock vibrate with the notes, and then it shattered.

Devis charged the door, which swung open in a cloud of sparkling black shards that had once been the stone lock. The lead dwarf barely got his head raised when Devis released the spell, and the heavy bars of the door hit the dwarf full in the face. Blood spouted from his broken nose, and he toppled backward.

The armored elf flipped his guard into the air with a jerk and flopped the dwarf onto his back. Before Devis could say a word, the elf produced a gleaming short sword from behind his back—the bard glimpsed some very old Elvish script on the blade—and raised the weapon over the cowering guard.

"No!" the bard cried, grabbing the elf's wrist with both hands and keeping the sword in the air. "We don't need a murder charge on our heads. We can get out without killing anybody."

The seething elf turned and met Devis's gaze. The bard didn't flinch. "Look—" he realized he had no idea what to call the man, but pressed on anyway, "—friend, I don't know you, but here we are." The dwarf on the ground whimpered, pinned by the armored elf's knees. "It's time to go.

"Am I wrong? Are you a murderer?" Devis asked the elf. The other man shook his head. "No kill dwarf," Devis offered.

"Yes," the elf said, a veneer of sanity returning to his face. "No kill," he added in a peculiar accent Devis couldn't quite place.

The dwarf on the ground struggled, and the elf brought the pommel down hard across the guard's jaw. The dwarf fell silent, still breathing.

"See how easy that was?" Devis asked.

He collected the guards' weapons, but had one leftover axe.

Devis carried the axe down the cell block until he found a familiar voice. He tossed the axe onto the floor in front of the burly half-orc.

"Can you chop your way out?"

"Shaddup, bard," the half-orc growled, but he quickly snapped up the axe.

Devis dashed back to his new ally and the unconscious guards. Devis briefly considered stealing a pair of boots, but the guard's footwear would not have fit Mialee, let alone him. With the elf's help, he pulled the inert guards into his cell and closed the door with its shattered lock.

The ring of steel on stone rebounded down the cell block. The half-orc had accepted the challenge.

Devis and the mystery elf dashed up the stairs.

The cacophony at the town lock-up was still ringing in the distance as the two escapees stepped from one of a thousand dark alleyways crisscrossing the south side of Dogmar.

The elf sniffed the air, then took off at a brisk walk down the muddy street. The rain had finally settled into a light drizzle, but Devis couldn't bring himself to believe the elf was really planning to follow his nose. Still, they had to go somewhere.

"So, what's your name?" Devis asked as he caught up to the quiet elf.

"Don't know," the elf replied.

"Really. That can't be easy. I've got to have something to call you." Devis considered. "You're as silent as stone. How about 'Diir'?"

"Diir," the elf said, " 'Stone.' Yes."

"Great! See, we're already getting along famously," Devis said. "So what brings you into the good graces of Constable Muhn, Diir?"

"Mialee," the elf replied.

"Ah. I've never been to—Mialee?" Devis pulled in front of the armored elf and stopped him with a finger to the chest. "How do you know Mialee?"

The elf looked past Devis down the street as he answered, "Find Mialee. Old man said so."

"How do you know she's here?" Devis asked. He looked back over his shoulder. "And what old man, exactly?" he added. Mialee had been waiting for an old elf.

"Old elf. Got hurt," the elf replied as he maneuvered around Devis and continued walking.

Devis pressed two fingers to his temple and vowed to go easy on Gurgitt's house ale from now on. And to have more respect for jailhouse coincidences.

"I can help you find Mialee," Devis said, catching up to the elf. "We'll need to find her quickly. That riot can't last much longer, and we're wanted men. This way." Devis angled the quiet elf in the direction of the Silver Goblet. "Keep an eye out for town guardsmen the farther north we get."

"Wrong way," the elf said.

"You'll end up too far north if you go that way."

"It's the wrong way," Diir insisted.

"All right, look. If I'm wrong, we'll only have gone maybe a half hour out of our way," Devis said.

"Lead," said the elf.

"Right," the bard acknowledged. "It's not far."

The rain had just begun to let up when Mialee arrived at the Temple of the Protector.

The entire structure looked like the stump of a single, enormous tree, but the elf woman could spot the seams where wood had been expertly worked together while still alive to give the illusion of a solid surface. The wide doors swung outward as she walked up white stone steps. Torches adorning the carved walls beckoned invitingly, as did the blast of warmth.

"It seems we've come at a bad time, Mialee," Biksel said from above.

Mialee stepped between the doors into the cozy torchlight and saw what her familiar meant. The temple appeared empty.

Mialee moved on cat feet through the torchlit space. She opened her hands to let the injured bird take in the surroundings. If the raven was what she suspected. . . .

The bird chirped weakly, but did not speak.

The doors swung shut behind them with a creak.

A crash and several thumps rang from above, falling steadily downward. She spied an archway cut into the wood that led up a spiral staircase. As she watched, a small figure in blue robes tumbled to a stop at the bottom of the stairs.

"Welcome, pilgrims!" a high-pitched voice squealed from the resulting pile of blue robes at the foot of the steps. The figure struggled to her feet, shifting a large leather bag on her hip that clanked with the sound of glass on glass. Mialee noted with surprise that she was looking at a grinning gnome woman who wore the full vestment of a cleric of Corellon Larethian, the Protector.

"With all due respect," Biksel said to the gnome, "the only true clerics of the Protector are elves."

"Biksel," Mialee snapped, then bowed slightly to the gnome. "I am Mialee. I need your help."

The cleric seemed taken aback by her bluntness, or perhaps by the fact that Mialee did not question why a gnome was the only denizen of an elven temple.

"Uh, all right," the gnome said. "You came to the right place! I am Zalyn, cleric of the Protector. I see you are bleeding." The gnome fumbled around in her oversized leather bag and produced a small vial.

Mialee blinked, then remembered that she was wet, bloody, and naked. "No, not me," she corrected, and shoved the wounded raven's tiny body under the cleric's nose. "This is . . . well, I'm not sure who she is."

"The poor thing." The cleric tucked the potion away and extended her cupped hands. Mialee gently slid the battered bird into Zalyn's palms.

The gnome spoke in Elvish and raised cupped hands toward the large silver crescent. A moment passed, and she lowered her hands. "It worked!" the cleric whispered.

In the gnome's palms sat a completely healthy raven, dozing peacefully. "She'll need a few minutes to wake up, I'd guess," Zalyn whispered as Mialee took the raven into her hands. The cleric examined the elf woman. "Sure I can't help you? That's a nasty wound on your forehead. And, well, isn't it cold out there? I'm sure I have a spare robe somewhere." The gnome dashed back up the spiral staircase.

The elf woman was staring at the sleeping bird. She made a mental promise to spend a week studying divine magic after she got to the bottom of Favrid's disappearance.

"Mialee," Biksel squawked, "our charge has recovered. However, you must attend to yourself. You're shivering."

Zalyn reappeared at the bottom of the stairs, holding up a golden robe that dragged on the wooden steps. "I believe this should fit you, friend Mialee," the cleric offered.

Even though the robe dragged on the floor as Zalyn held it up, Mialee could see it was still very small. The wizard was tall for an elf. Were there no spare elf-sized clothes in this elven temple? Still, it beat the nothing she was wearing at the moment.

The fabric felt strange, but immediately warmed her skin.

"And now for your forehead. Let's see...." Zalyn fumbled in her large bag and produced a scroll. Her mouth moved silently as she went over whatever incantation was written on the document.

Satisfied, Zalyn rolled up the scroll and stowed it in her shoulder bag. "Mialee, if you please," she beckoned. Mialee leaned down so the gnome could reach her injured forehead.

Zalyn whispered another prayer and pressed her palms on either side of the wizard's temple. Mialee waited for the familiar warm tingle of magical healing. And waited.

Nothing happened. The elf waited, and the gnome whispered another soft prayer.

After a full minute, Mialee pulled back. Zalyn shook her head and stared at her hands, then looked intently at Mialee's wound again. She muttered another prayer and thrust the silver crescent around her neck at the elf woman.

Mialee felt a single drop of blood run down between her eyes and onto the tip of her nose. "I don't think it's working," she said.

"I don't understand." The gnome's voice was tinged with frustration. She held the holy crescent in both hands and intoned loudly, "By the power of Corellon Larethian, this wound is healed!"

Mialee touched her forehead. Her fingers came away sticky and red. She sighed. "Zalyn, please. I'll be OK. Maybe a potion?"

"Yes, of course," Zalyn replied. Disappointment covered her face like a mask, but the gnome produced a tiny vial and handed it to Mialee. "Drink this. Normally, I'd recommend a topical salve, I guess, but . . ."

Mialee snatched the vial, popped the seal, and quaffed the potion before Zalyn could finish. The elf woman felt a tingle on her forehead and wiped her brow with the back of her arm. She gently touched the spot where the raven had collided with her. The skin felt solid.

"Thanks," Mialee said. She threw a glance at the tiny raven slumbering under the icon of the Protector. "How long will we have to wait?"

"I can't say for sure," Zalyn said. "I've never seen something that took such a beating and lived. And a good thing it did, too."

"What do you mean?" Biksel interrupted.

"I think she means that she hasn't yet learned to raise the dead," Mialee said. "Would that be correct, Zalyn?"

"Er, yes," the gnome said sheepishly.

"Why are you the only one in this temple?" Biksel asked.

"The others left. A week ago," Zalyn said. "They headed south."

"Why not you?" Mialee said.

"They didn't need me. 'We've got plenty of rations, and we'll be back by sundown,' the master said. 'You keep watch here. We've no need for a cook,' he said. Happens all the time, frankly."

"You're the cook?" Biksel and Mialee asked simultaneously.

"Not just a cook!" Zalyn objected defiantly. "I study, I learn, I follow the Protector!" The gnome turned her gaze to the floor. "Between meals. But you saw it; I can summon the healing magic."

As if in support, a faint but healthy squawk came from the raven on the pedestal.

"Mialee," the bird said. Its voice was surprisingly soothing. "You are Mialee?"

The elf woman nodded as the bird settled into a perch on the edge of the pedestal. The raven cocked an eye at Mialee's familiar. "And you must be Biksel. Favrid warned me about you. You're rather arrogant, he says."

"Typical," Biksel sniffed.

"Favrid?" Mialee interjected. "Are you his new familiar? Where is he? He was supposed to meet me days ago!"

"I am Favrid's fourth familiar. He summoned me into his service ten years ago, after the death of Ama, my predecessor. I am called Darji," the smaller raven said.

"Where is Favrid, Darji?" Biksel said impatiently.

Darji shuddered. "A bad place," she managed, "but he must be alive."

Mialee opened her mouth to ask another question when they all heard the crash of breaking glass from up the spiral staircase.

"What the——?" Mialee managed.

Darji leaped into the air from the pedestal and started circling the inside of the temple. "I'm sorry," she squawked as she spun overhead, "but I think they've found me."

Zalyn screamed as a dozen flapping shapes with hollow black eye sockets and white-tufted necks exploded from the archway and filled the room with acrid stench. Darkness enveloped Mialee as the torchlight guttered out.

"Not much better," Devis said, examining his attire. "But it beats the alternative."

Money was in short supply for the two fugitives, but Devis had scrounged enough for a tunic, pants, and boots. He regretted giving up a weapon in his current situation, but had to admit it was a pretty good deal. He had been able to get a few pieces of gold for the dwarven axe. Neither he nor Diir wanted to part with the crossbows; Devis because he was actually a decent shot with the weapon, Diir for his own, undisclosed reasons.

The money was enough to buy the clothes and one other item besides. The bard absently struck a ringing chord on his cheap, used lute.

It, too, beat the alternative.

The rain had stopped completely, and the clouds had finally broken to let beams of warm sunlight cut the morning chill in the autumn air. Devis noodled an old favorite on the lute as he walked along.

The telltale sign of the Silver Goblet appeared as they rounded a bend in the street. "No sign of the town guard," Devis said, not really expecting an answer.

Diir sniffed the air and nodded.

"Glad you agree," Devis said. "Now let's find out what you and my friend Mialee have in common, shall we?"

They emerged from the Silver Goblet ten minutes later.

Devis couldn't understand it. Gurgitt had been more than happy to let him into Mialee's room, especially after Devis charmed the innkeeper with a song-spell and one of their precious gold pieces. What they found only baffled Devis further.

It might have all made perfect sense to Diir, but the elf didn't say so. He simply insisted that Mialee was not in the room—which was obvious—and that Devis should follow him.

They'd found the door to Mialee's room wide open, as were the shutters on her window. Devis's clothing and gear were still scattered across the floor, along with his equipment and all of the gold he'd won from Muhn, which he was glad to recover. The bard also retrieved his thick leather vest and trusty long sword, which now hung from his belt. But strangely, all of Mialee's things were still there, too, including her rapier, wand, spellbook, and magical components.

She'd simply disappeared. The bird was gone, too. Fortunately, nothing indicated another wight attack, which was a relief. But had Muhn succeeded in capturing the girl?

Devis swung the lute around to his back and pulled the small leather pouch from his belt. Mialee had insisted that the pockets on the pouch held birdseed, but Devis knew enough about wizards to realize that was a bald-faced lie. He hadn't had time to grab anything else except a papyrus scroll that confirmed Mialee's story about her missing teacher.

Diir broke into a jog as they neared the northern edge of Dogmar, and Devis had to run to keep up. The elf was leading them to a large, wooden building of undeniable elven manufacture, all curved, golden timber and smooth, polished surfaces. A silver crescent four times as tall as Devis crowned the three-story structure.

"The Temple of the Protector?" he exclaimed. "She's that hung over?"

"Inside," Diir replied.

"Maybe you should go first."

Before Diir could move, the doors swung open and a dozen flapping shapes poured out of the open doors. Vultures, Devis realized, but unlike any he'd ever seen.

Judging from their appearance, these vultures were dead.

The horrid, flapping creatures immediately set upon Diir, who whirled and sliced at his attackers with his short sword. Two twitching, feathered corpses splattered to the ground in four pieces, but the rest fled, screeching through torn throats.

"Where is the other?" the wolf's master snarled in the lupine tongue.

"Elf with burning tooth," the wolf growled in reply. "Tooth bites head. Burns my neck."

"The elf escaped?" the master asked.

"Yes," the wolf admitted, "but it says word."

"What word?"

"Elf-talk," the wolf replied.

"I see." The figure on the carved stone throne clasped its hands and concentrated in the orange glow of torches, then placed two bony fingertips on the wolf's ears.

"Speak," the wolf's master commanded in Elvish.

The wolf barked and growled in an approximation of the ancient language of the forests, though it did not comprehend how. "Elf says, 'Mialee'."

"Nothing else?"

"Nothing," the wolf barked.

The wolf's master turned to the tortured figure hanging from the wall. "Favrid, old friend," the master growled, "whatever have you been up to?"

The rest of the conversation became incomprehensible to the wolf as its master's spell faded, so the drooling creature busied itself with the delectable pool of scarlet blood collecting beneath the master's prisoner.

Devis's jaw dropped. Before him stood a tiny gnome, small even by the standards of her own people. She held a silver crescent, the mirror image of the icon atop the temple, in two shaking fists. Sweat covered the gnome's dark face and she gasped for air like she'd just run ten leagues.

From the darkness behind the gnome, a lithe, familiar figure stepped into the light. She wore what looked like a gnome-sized set of golden robes that scintillated in the morning sun, and a raven was perched on each dusky shoulder.

"Devis," Mialee said.

"Um, hi," Devis offered lamely.

"Did you see it, Mialee?" the gnome interrupted. "Only a true servant of the Protector could have done that. I turned the undead! I saved the temple!"

To Devis's surprise, Diir suddenly joined the conversation.

"Mialee," he said to the elf woman, and bowed deeply.

"Yes, she's Mialee," the larger of the two ravens, Mialee's familiar, replied. "Who are you?"

47

"He doesn't know," Devis cut in. "It's a long story. What happened to you?"

"What happened to you?" the wizard shot back.

"In fact, I got locked up in the —"

"Excuse me," the gnome interjected. "Perhaps we should move inside. I don't know what those things did to my kitchen, and who knows when they'll decide to come back?"

"I haven't eaten this well in days, Zalyn," Devis said as he soaked up the last of his stew with a piece of fresh bread. "Remind me to slip something into the offering box on my way out."

"Thank you, Zalyn. It was wonderful," Mialee said

"Good," blurted Diir. "Thanks."

The gnome scuttled over to the low table with a teapot nearly twice the size of her head and filled four cups. "It's a pleasure," Zalyn said with pride. "It's rare that I get a chance to make anything out of the ordinary, if you take my meaning, especially for guests."

"They don't know what they're missing," said Devis.

Zalyn blushed and returned to her bubbling pots.

A corner of Mialee's mind went over what Darji had told her. She found it difficult to believe the familiar's bizarre story. The raven had accompanied Favrid from the southern deserts after Favrid discovered something that agitated him greatly. Darji said she didn't understand what the discovery was, but it had something to do with a tomb, another contrived prophecy, and a battle Favrid had fought in long ago.

Darji and Favrid had traveled north with a caravan of traders to an elven village nestled in the forest, a place called Silatham. Devis scoffed at the idea of the mythical lost outpost, but didn't say much more. His eyes almost flashed gold as Mialee saw him mentally calculate how much the location of a lost legend could be worth to the right people.

Favrid and his familiar visited the halfling Tent City Devis had told her about earlier and explored into the Morkeryth ruins. Darji remembered nothing between entering the ruins and waking up in the temple.

Mialee still wasn't sure what to make of the bard. She found him pleasant enough, but she also suspected his motives. Devis didn't strike her as the sort of man who did anything without expecting a return.

This other elf, Diir, was a baffling mystery. His accent, when he bothered to speak at all, reminded her of the dignified speech of a royal court.

He had hardly said another word since calling her by name. Mialee took a sip of Zalyn's tea and decided it was time to pry a little more information out of the reticent elf. With Darji's memory blanked out, Diir might be her only link to Favrid. Mialee hated not knowing what was going on.

She decided on a direct approach. "Diir," she said, "you seem to know who I am, but I don't believe we've ever met. Do you know Favrid?"

The elf frowned. When he spoke, he pronounced each word deliberately, as if trying it out for the first time. "Favrid. Old elf, Mialee?"

Mialee nearly choked on her herbal tea. "Yes! An old elf! Do you know him?" she demanded. Devis and Zalyn both stopped what they were doing and looked expectantly at Diir.

"Don't know," the elf said, frustration showing, "Don't know anything . . . useful. Just old man. Said find Mialee."

"So you saw him recently?" Mialee pressed.

"Yes," Diir replied. "I remember the old man." The more he spoke, the more easily the words seemed to come. His accent remained strange, however. "And . . . a thing. Bony. Red eyes, and voice like knives."

The wizard shook her head. "He can't be dead. Darji couldn't talk to us if he was dead."

"You ran?" Devis jumped in again. "Diir, I haven't known you for long, but you don't strike me as the type to run from anything."

"Didn't want to. It . . . something . . ." The elf dug for the right word. "Compelled me," he finished, rolling the word over his tongue and casting a glance at Zalyn. He turned intently to Mialee, who was surprised at how agitated the quiet man had become. "I did not want to run. But when he told me to go. . . .'"

"It wasn't your fault, Diir," said Mialee, while Devis blinked at the flood of words from his taciturn companion. "I think you may have been enchanted. Favrid commanded you."

"If you'll pardon me, Mialee," Zalyn said over her shoulder, "I don't see what the mystery is. Your old teacher was having trouble and needed your help."

"But why me?" Mialee said. "I'm a neophyte compared to some of the mages he consorts with."

"Perhaps he didn't need someone powerful," Zalyn replied gently. "Perhaps he simply needed someone he could trust."

Trust. Mialee felt a warm wave of shame wash over her features, and she blushed. The realization of her selfishness over the past couple of days hit her full in the face like a cart full of bricks. Despite the obvious and immediate threat of the undead, she'd been more concerned with Favrid's bad manners, the long journey he'd demanded of her, and his failure to keep a schedule.

Devis spoke next. "Well, I've heard enough," he said, pushing back from the table and rising to his feet. "Mialee, you need to find this old man, and you need a guide. I told you before, I know that area, and it can be risky. Diir, are you with us?"

The elf nodded.

Mialee had a thought. "Diir, do you know if Favrid cast any other spells on you besides the one that compelled you to find me?"

"Don't know," the elf said in his peculiar accent, shrugging. "Didn't know he cast the first one."

"What are you thinking, Mialee?" Devis asked, turning back from the window. "Did Favrid enchant Diir's sword?"

"Maybe," Mialee said without looking at the bard. "Or maybe it's something more than that. Diir, may I cast a simple spell of magical detection on you?"

The elf thought for a moment, then shrugged again. "Please."

Mialee waved her hands with a brief series of sharp, quick motions and softly whispered, "*Hinual, lerret.*"

"Wish I'd thought of that," Devis muttered.

The spell opened her senses gradually to the presence of magic in the area. Mialee coaxed the effect around Diir.

The elf's short sword glowed blood red in her altered vision. Mialee did her best to explain to the others what she was seeing. "Strong conjurative magic in the sword," she reported. "Maybe some type of bane. And something else . . ." she trailed off.

Another magical field, so faint she'd almost missed it, suffused the elf's entire body. The intensity of the field was most powerful in and around Diir's head, but traces of it glowed softly from the elf's head to his boots.

The magic was transmutative. Something had recently altered Diir at the most basic level, but the job hadn't quite been completed.

The elf's head, inexplicably, was made of something different from the rest of his body.

"Mialee, what is it?" Zalyn asked.

The wizard let the spell lapse. She'd learned all she could from it.

"What did you see?" Devis asked.

Mialee ignored the bard and placed a hand on Diir's shoulder. "Diir, I'm not sure how to explain it," she said, "but I think part of your head is made of, well, stone."

Devis laughed uncontrollably and had to hold himself up on a chair. "Stone is a stone? Are you serious?"

Mialee stared at him. "Completely," she said, turning to look Diir in the eye. "I'm not saying it makes sense," the wizard explained, "but I can only think of two possibilities—either some-one or some thing is trying to turn you into your namesake—"

"Or?" Diir asked.

"Or you were once turned to stone, and whoever changed you back didn't quite finish the transformation," said Mialee. "I said it didn't make much sense. I've seen statues come to life before, and never once has one of them demanded to know who it was."

Mialee swept her gaze around the room and finally let her eyes meet with the bard's. "I'll take you up on your offer, Devis. Diir, if you'll still join us, there's a chance we can restore your memory, if Favrid survives. The spell is beyond my skill, but that old man has forgotten more arcane art than the Blue Order ever knew."

Diir nodded.

Devis sobered. "It's going to be dangerous, Mialee," he said with no hint of teasing or jest. "Is this old man worth it?"

"I'm through worrying about myself. I've been doing far too much of that lately," Mialee said, strapping her rapier to her belt. She picked up her traveling pack and slung it over her shoulders.

Zalyn emerged from the kitchen with a clank of vials and scur-ried about the room handing each of them a pack of still-warm rations. "We'll need something to eat, I imagine," she said.

"Zalyn, who will look after the temple?" said Mialee.

A flutter of wings made all of them start, and two ravens lit on Mialee. "I would be honored, Zalyn, to look after the affairs of the

Temple of the Protector." Zalyn blinked as the bird actually approximated a bow.

"Biksel, no offense, but that's ridiculous," said Devis. "You can't even lift the lid on the offering box."

"Is somebody talking?" Biksel cawed. "Mialee, Darji and I may be small, but I resent the implication that we would be unable to summon help should a gang of bandits storm the temple." The raven cocked an eye at the gnome. "The front door, that's a permanent spell, isn't it?"

"What? Oh, yes. Completely automatic. Opens right up for anybody who wants to enter," Zalyn offered. "Well, that's not entirely true. There's all kinds of wards and protections against ghouls, vampires, wild animals, the constable—"

"Biksel," said Mialee, "I need you."

"I won't be far," the raven said. "But you know I would be more of a hindrance than a help. I do not speak selfishly when I say my death at a critical moment could impact you strongly enough to get you killed. You may not be able to protect me, and therefore you may not be able to protect yourself."

"He really can handle this place for a day or two, I'm sure of it, Mialee," Zalyn said.

"Yes, you must stay here, Biksel," said a female voice that was not Mialee's. Darji flapped from Mialee's shoulder and lit on the windowsill next to Devis. "And I must go with them."

"Out of the question," Biksel squawked.

"She's right," Mialee said. "She's our connection to Favrid."

"Mialee, I choose freely to accompany you, and in return I ask only one thing. If I become . . . if I revert to an animal state," the little raven chirped, "you will turn back. We know there are things in Morkeryth worse than vultures or wolves. You warned me of the creature you faced in the tavern. If Favrid is dead. . . ."

"If that happens, Darji, I promise I will consider it. But I'm not the only one with a voice in this." She lifted a hand to indicate the rest of the assembled group. "Diir's got rocks in his head. Zalyn serves the Protector. Devis will rob the temple blind if we don't take him with us."

"Hey," Devis said.

"You would."

"Oh, dear," Zalyn said, and dropped her leather bag to the floor with a jingle of vials as she dashed back into her kitchen. The gnome began flinging cupboards open, muttering to herself.

"Zalyn?" Devis called. "I think we have plenty of rations. More than plenty," he added. He held a hand to his stomach, where two extra helpings of pepper stew were exacting vengeance.

"No," Zalyn shouted. "No!"

The gnome ran back into the dining room, clutching a piece of yellow parchment. "What you said about serving the Protector, it reminded me. The brothers, they left this note. 'If something happens so disastrous that you must flee, find us in Silatham'."

"Silatham," Diir said. "We'll pass right by it on the way to the mountain. I'm sure of it."

"Yes!" Zalyn said, running over to the elf and pushing the parchment under his nose. "Like the bird said, an elf village, down south of Morsilath in the deep woods. Very mysterious. Don't seem to like other people. But it's just a stone's throw from Morkeryth, as I understand. You know it?"

"I do," Diir said. "I think it's my home."

Devis blinked at Diir's casual revelation. "Home?" the bard asked. Diir might as well have announced he was a bugbear.

"If there's trouble involving the dead things, the brothers have to know about it." Zalyn shivered. "Maybe they already do. If there's something out there stronger than all the brothers combined . . ."

"We'll find out," Mialee said.

"Yes, find out," Biksel said. "I wish to assume my post, and the five of you are cluttering up the Temple of the Protector."

The rat on his shoulder chattered into the wight's ear. A wicked grin spread over the leathery gray countenance, and red eyes flashed with fire. Wiry hair flew back behind his head and tattered robes flapped as the mine car sped down the long-abandoned shaft.

The tracks on the long tunnel would carry the wight underground, far north of his mountain prison. A thousand years ago, carts like this ran from mines on the south slope of Morsilath all the way to Dogmar. After his defeat a millennium ago, the tunnels had been sealed off several miles south of the town, but no one had bothered or dared to block the southern ends of the tunnels.

It had taken Cavadrec only a few centuries to learn that his imprisonment was not complete. His enemies had woefully underestimated the wight's patience, to say nothing of the power hidden deep inside Morsilath.

"Very good," Cavadrec told the hollow-eyed rodent. "You and your kin have brought the first generation of our wightling horde into being."

The last word whistled from the wight's hissing mouth in the strong wind. The rat squeaked a reply in rat-talk and scrambled down the back of the wight's torn rags to leap into the darkness.

Cavadrec twisted his head around one hundred and eighty degrees to watch the rat land violently on the tracks and roll like a furry sausage until it tumbled to a stop. Such a feat would have left an ordinary animal smeared on the floor of the long tunnel, but Cavadrec's pets were made of sterner stuff.

The wight stretched out a sinewy arm. A gnarled staff of black wood snapped from the floor of the cart into his open hand. He turned the head of the staff so that the empty sockets of the skull atop the staff stared into his own red eyes. Cavadrec hissed an invocation.

He felt his consciousness split. Half of Cavadrec's mind left his body and stretched south, racing through miles of rock and spreading into the roiling waters of the river Mormsilath. A primitive reptilian mind welcomed its master's presence.

Cavadrec settled into the brain of the creature and a dark, hulking shape left the floor of the riverbed in a swirl of green-brown silt.

The infestation of Silatham was only the beginning. Now, he needed just a few random travelers snatched from the busy road.

"Devis, the sun's past noon. What are you doing out there?" Mialee shouted into the woods. She stood along the dirt road that cut through the thick evergreen forest of Silath. She sighed and gazed with frustration at the sky. Only a few dozen yards to their south, a wide, wooden bridge arched over the river Mormsilath. The roar of rushing water filled the air, and cool mist twinkled with tiny rainbows in the sun. The clouds had burned off completely.

Zalyn and Diir stood packed and ready to cross the bridge, both as able as they'd been just a few hours ago. It was their second day on the road.

"Just a minute!" Devis whispered theatrically. Mialee guessed he was maybe twenty feet away. "And keep it down! Don't you know there are wolves in these woods?"

"I can barely hear you," the wizard called back. She briefly considered whether to send Darji after the bard to make sure he hadn't walked into a wolf trap.

Mialee sighed and shifted in her new clothing. She hoped it would stop pinching soon. The robe didn't fit yet, but it was getting there. The long branches of magically treated athel wood forming the ribs of the protective garment would slowly curve to fit her body, but needed a little more time.

The robe was over two thousand years old, Zalyn had told her, and belonged to one of the dozens of legendary heroes of the order. The outfit had been the first thing Mialee spotted when they ventured below the temple to the armory. She had seen a similar garment only once before, in a remote elf village far to the north where contact with other races was limited and metal was scarce. Curved plates of athel wood projected from the shoulders. The curious, lightweight fibers would supposedly bounce any blow off of Mialee and back at the attacker. The high collar, also made of athel, would block a blade aimed at her throat, while athel-sapling ribs in the corset-like lower section protected her below the neck.

The elf tested the string of her new longbow with one finger and released it. The bowstring twanged a clear musical note, a sure sign of the weapon's masterful elven make. Mialee accepted the bow only after Zalyn insisted. She didn't feel right taking so much from the temple, but Zalyn assured her that the weapons were there to fight evil.

Their mysterious amnesiac still carried his short sword, but had added a simple long sword, an intricately carved leather weapons belt, and a lightweight helm selected from the temple's armory.

Devis carried a dagger that looked extremely valuable, insisting many times that "the heft felt just right." More importantly, he also had a new elven crossbow and his old long sword and leather armor.

Zalyn had not overlooked herself when the weapons were parceled out. When the gnome proudly walked out in what she called "full battle dress," Mialee had been forced to stifle a laugh.

Zalyn gleamed in the afternoon sun. Her helm bore an upturned crescent and an improbable plume of blue feathers. Her silver breastplate carried the same crescent, and to Mialee's surprise, actually fit Zalyn like a glove.

Zalyn confessed that she'd had her eye on the armor for months, ever since discovering it in the armory. Mialee didn't ask why a temple serving elves would have such tiny armor. Zalyn seemed to think it was the will of Corellon Larethian, and the wizard was loath to contradict her. For all Mialee knew, it was.

The little raven flapped down from a nearby branch to settle on one athel wood flange next to Mialee's ear.

"Would you like me to scout the bridge, Mialee?" Darji asked.

"Not alone, Darji," Mialee said, shaking her head. "But thanks for offering. It's a good idea." Although she could not commune with Favrid's familiar, the little bird often seemed to be reading her mind.

The wizard peered toward the bridge and slung the longbow onto her back. She glanced back toward the tree line.

"Devis," she called, "Darji wants to scout the bridge, but I'm not letting her go alone. Catch up with us, we'll wait there."

"Sure, fine," the bard whispered loudly somewhere in the dark woods.

The trio set out down the road when a tremendous splash erupted ahead of them, loud enough to drown out the roar of the river itself. Mialee, Zalyn, and Diir broke into a run at the sound and Darji took flight.

"Hey, what was that?" Devis hissed from the trees, but his companions were already out of earshot.

Devis was still buckling his sword belt as he burst from the trees onto the road. The others were already at the bridge, but at this distance he could scarcely make them out through the mist. The river was kicking up a lot more moisture than it had been when horrible indigestion forced the bard into the woods. He ran through the cold vapor to join his companions.

He arrived in time to see Mialee dive to one side and an arrow cut through the air where her head had been a half-second before.

"Ambush!" Zalyn cried, drawing her short sword.

"Ambush?" Devis shouted over the roar of the river, quickly scanning the roiling water. "What made that splash?"

None of his companions was in any position to answer, and within seconds Devis forgot the question. A volley of arrows shot out from the forest on the north shore of the river Mormsilath, forcing the party to scatter onto the bridge.

Devis heard Mialee whisper a spell as Darji took to the air. The bard saw a faint blue glow enshroud the elf woman for a moment. The aura soaked into the wizard's skin and disappeared.

A personal armor field, he guessed. Smart move. Mialee's skimpy, borrowed robe barely protected her from fatal sunburn, let alone a speeding arrow. He sung a quick refrain and felt a similar magical field surround his own body.

Diir already held both swords in his hands and was scanning the tree line.

The bard stooped to pick up one of the projectiles while keeping his eye on the north shore. He recognized the make immediately. He'd seen the like a hundred times in the tent city on Morkeryth.

Something inside Devis snapped.

The bard had tried to live a good life, if only on the fringe of polite society. He'd befriended the downtrodden. He'd never resorted to blood to settle a dispute unless he was given no other choice. And when he did dip into the odd temple treasury or innkeeper's cashbox, he always made sure to spread a little of the wealth to those less fortunate than himself.

Yesterday, all Devis wanted to do was impress the pretty girl and maybe coax her back into one of the private rooms at the Silver Goblet. He didn't deserve this final insult. The god of the open road had abandoned his balladeer. Devis was under attack by halfling highwaymen.

His companions could only stare as the bard stomped back the way they had come, an arrow clutched in his white-knuckled fist.

"All right, you idiots!" Devis shouted at the forest as he neared the end of the wooden slats. Another hail of arrows erupted from the trees, sending Mialee, Diir, and Zalyn running for cover that wasn't there. Devis continued off the bridge and strode with grim purpose to the tree line, ignoring the volley of deadly projectiles. By dumb luck, all the arrows missed him but one. That shaft should have struck him, but it deflected away as if by magic.

The bard stopped, placed one hand on his sword hilt, and shook the arrow in his fist at the unseen attackers. "Who's out there?" Devis hollered at the top of his lungs. The bard hurled the arrow into the trees and drew his sword. He raised the blade over his head like a pirate king and snarled, "YOU CAN ALL GO TO HELL!"

Water roared in Devis' ears. High overhead, Darji cawed. A wolf howled somewhere in the forest, far south of the river.

"Devis?" a small, hesitant voice called from the tree line. A tiny figure, only slightly larger than Zalyn, stepped from the shadow-ridden woods. The halfling held a short bow in one hand. He wore simple, homespun clothes, a quiver, a dagger, and a familiar cloak of not-quite-cured animal hides. One eye was covered by a thick leather patch made from a dog's ear.

"Hound-Eye?" Devis laughed.

Hound-Eye didn't answer, merely stared intently at Devis with one eye. Someone had reattached his foot, but the halfling stood at an angle that told the bard an expert had not done the job. Devis had never seen Hound-Eye look so deadly serious. Two more half-lings emerged, flanking the man Devis had known as a petty thief. He recognized the two new arrivals.

The female in the wolfskin tunic was called Takata. She ran with a gang that fancied themselves wild bandits of the forest, but her base was in Tent City. She was a powerful figure in the community, bringing stolen goods and pilfered wealth into the makeshift village at an admirable profit. What most people didn't know was that Hound-Eye and Takata were married and had two young children. The male in the improbably bright velvet suit Devis knew only as Bloody Bill. He and his well-dressed outfit ran the other half of Tent City, specializing in blackmail, gambling, and assassination.

Something had drastically shaken up the status quo. These

were pillars of the community, relatively speaking. Why had they taken to the open road like common bandits?

"Well?" Devis asked. "What are you doing this far south? Bill, you need a new suit?"

Hound-Eye looked to his left and right, then cleared his throat. "It's gone, Devis," he said with genuine sadness. "All of it. We're all that's left."

"What's gone?" Devis's voice trailed off as understanding intruded. His hunch had been right, unfortunately. "Oh. Oh, gods. Hound-Eye." He waved his sword and said more clearly, "All of you. I'm so sorry." The bard swallowed. "How did it happen?" he asked. He already knew the answer. "Undead?"

"Wolves," the one-eyed thief said. "Not normal ones."

"They devoured our families whole," Bloody Bill growled. "Nothing could stop them. They didn't feel pain."

"Or fear," Takata added. "I'd never met a wolf I couldn't scare off before today, or a wight I couldn't kill. We get both wandering into Tent City all the time. These were something else."

"Of course they were something else!" Hound-Eye barked. "They were both!"

"Excuse me," Zalyn interrupted from behind Devis. She strode fearlessly forward, oversized shoulder bag clanking against her shining armor with each step, and deliberately pulled off her leather gloves and dropped them onto the bridge. "I am a healer. Please, I can help your wounded." She raised her hands to show her empty palms. "I bear you no ill will, or, um, anything like that."

The last thing Devis expected to see next was an enormous, black crocodile with empty eye sockets explode from the river and charge onto the bank straight at the hapless halflings. But he did.

The survivors of Tent City screamed and scattered, but the croc—a thirty-footer, at least—moved with supernatural speed and it snapped up Bloody Bill in one gulp.

The bank of the river shook as the huge crocodile swiveled its massive body on the narrow beach. White foam shot high into the air as the creature's broad tail cut across the water's surface. The crocodile snorted, a curious noise that sounded less like an animal and far more like a disgusted three-year-old.

Devis had to be hallucinating. For just a moment, he actually thought the croc's empty sockets flashed twin pinpricks of blood-red light.

And had the crocodile just grinned at him?

Diir's voice cut through the roar of the river and snapped Devis out of his trance.

"Bridge!" the elf cried.

Devis just managed to avoid several collisions as he turned to run south onto the wooden span. The crocodile followed him with its nose. For a split-second Devis thought the creature might simply return to the river, but the bridge shuddered violently as the massive zombie crocodile heaved its bulk out onto the thick, wooden planks.

The crocodile took three steps onto the centuries-old span. Devis heard the ancient pylons groan under the reptile's weight. A crossbeam snapped with a deafening crack, and the east side of the bridge dropped a foot. Everyone on the bridge, Devis included, jerked violently to one side.

The crocodile lumbered closer. All four of its tree-trunk legs rested on the creaking structure, and its tail churned sand and spray into the air. Shockwaves shuddered through the bridge and sent everyone stumbling.

Devis lost his balance and landed hard on his solar plexus. The bard gasped for breath. He couldn't see a thing, and his ears felt stuffed with cotton.

He heard more beams and pylons cracking and dug into the wet wooden planks with the tips of his fingers. The bridge dipped like a swayback horse under the reptile's weight. Devis felt himself slipping toward the monstrous croc, plank by plank.

Then he felt a pair of strong arms hook him under the shoulders and drag him away from the monster. Devis raised his battered head and looked at Diir, who somehow maintained his balance on the crumbling bridge as he dragged the bard away from immediate harm. With a grunt, the elf heaved and tossed Devis to the south shore of the river with his free hand. The rough landing left him staring at Hound-Eye's fur-booted feet.

Diir shouted over the noise of rushing water and cracking timbers, "I've a plan. Hit it with everything on my word!"

Devis heard the ring of elven steel cut through the roar of the river. Diir, he guessed, had just drawn his magic short sword. He noted absently that his friend's vocabulary was growing by leaps and bounds.

The little gnome cleric scampered to his side with a clank of armor and loose vials. Zalyn helped raise the bard into a sitting position and knelt on the ground behind Devis to prop him up. As soon as Devis opened his eyes, he immediately wished Diir had left him to slide into the crocodile's belly. At least that would have been quick, and he would have known his friends had outlived him, if only for a few minutes.

He tucked his knees and pushed off with his palms, forcing his body forward, and rolled onto the balls of his feet. Zalyn grasped his hands before he could roll backward, and helped him stand.

Devis flicked a leather strap from his right shoulder. The battered lute dropped into his hand from the carrying strap he'd contrived from a "sling of protection" Zalyn pointed out in her non-stop travelogue through the temple armory. She promised it would deflect arrows, and apparently it had worked.

Devis winced as the convex body of the lute pressed against what was probably a broken rib, but he strummed a chord anyway. The sound was ugly and out of tune.

Without haste, Devis twisted a peg at the end of the lute's neck and plucked the offending string again, his focus on the crescendoing twang. He picked it twice, listened. Devis fretted the chord, hit each string in turn with his thumb. Then he picked up speed, plucking with flying fingers, now and then pausing to turn a peg or bend a lute string with his thumb, still in desperate pursuit of harmony.

Diir, Mialee, Takata, and Hound-Eye stood shoulder to shoulder in the cold spray at the edge of the bridge, staring down the gargantuan reptile. The crocodile now covered half the bridge, and what wooden planks remained behind the monster had been reduced to a tangled snarl of broken lumber. Hefty chunks of the structure had already broken free and floated downriver.

They needed inspiration. Devis launched into a ballad of ancient heroes, stalwart men and women standing tall, courageous in their resolve, the usual themes. He hated falling back on the standards, but circumstances didn't allow Devis the luxury of calling forth a new song from scratch, and in this case, the words of the music had very little to do with the magical effect he wanted.

The mist carried Devis's voice—cracking now and again, but serviceable—to his companions at the water's edge. Takata and Hound-Eye straightened and seemed to grow just a little bit taller as they held their short bows leveled at the croc, arrows nocked and ready. Diir twirled the gleaming, engraved short sword and shifted into a loose combat stance.

Mialee raised her right hand and Devis saw a ball of golden fire flare around her fingers.

Zalyn truly took Devis's song to heart. She loaded her small crossbow, pulled her feathered helm snugly over her head, and dashed past Devis to join the others with a war cry that made the bard's ears ring.

The remains of the shattered bridge cracked and popped with the crocodile's every shifting step. If the thing had been intelligent, Devis might have wondered if the creature was trying to drown out the bard's music with the cacophony of breaking lumber. The half-elf peered intently into the crocodile's black sockets through the swirling water spray.

Devis blinked and momentarily stopped strumming the lute. The crocodile's eyes had flashed blood red and the bard felt a blackness grip his soul. Devis's voice faltered, and he suddenly found himself fumbling for the lyrics to a fighting song he'd known since his eighth summer.

The bard wobbled with sudden vertigo and watched as his companions' resolve wilted. Zalyn visibly slumped in her armor, and the fire in Mialee's hand dimmed ever so slightly.

The crocodile chose that moment to charge, jaws flung wide. Jagged yellow teeth the size of a boar's tusks glinted in the filtered sunlight as the eyeless beast lumbered out of the mist. Heavy wooden slats snapped and flew into the foaming current as the croc's obsidian claws and considerable mass tore the bridge apart.

Diir held his ground and stared down the reptile's open gullet.

Devis felt an icy hand release his heart, and an entirely new ballad swelled inside him, demanding to be released. The words erupted uncontrollably and he swung his hand down to strike the lute strings so hard that his fingers bled. Devis's new tune magically drowned the sound of the river and the snarling, undead reptile that barreled snout-first toward the bard's most taciturn ally. He saw the others swell with martial pride.

Diir raised a gloved hand. The crocodile's jaws would close around him in seconds.

The elf's glove chopped the air. "Now!"

At his signal, Takata and Hound-Eye frantically pumped arrow after arrow into the creature's open maw. Zalyn's crossbow twanged and snapped as she fired and reloaded with surprising speed.

The bard rounded the second verse of his spontaneous melody and headed into the third movement.

Mialee shouted the last word of her spell and threw the ball of golden energy overhand into the crocodile's throat. The missile exploded and sizzled. Foul black smoke spread from the crocodile's jaws and mingled with spray from the raging river. Devis continued singing even as he lost sight of his companions in the haze.

Mialee and Takata emerged from one side of the cloud to Devis's left, while Zalyn and Hound-Eye circled out of the smog on Devis's right to flank the beast. Diir had disappeared.

No, there he is, Devis corrected himself as the monster's black-scaled jaws emerged, snarling, from the smog, followed by the rest of the enormous croc. Diir sat astride the crocodile's neck like a pixie on a warhorse. The bard backed away as quickly as he dared, leaving the third chorus behind and diving into an extended, improvisational bridge that let him lend some attention to where his feet were going.

The monster's jaws snapped shut with a deafening clap and the creature shook its neck like a wet dog, trying vainly to dislodge its unwanted rider. A real, living crocodile would have simply rolled into the water, but this undead creature seemed leery of exposing its underbelly to its opponents. The thing was fighting with intelligence, the bard realized, and hoped that Diir—who seemed to be a natural strategist and a hell of an acrobat—could hold on. Blast after blast of energy slammed into the creature's side from the tip of Mialee's wand while Zalyn and the halflings peppered the croc's thick hide with arrows.

Devis saw the croc-riding elf look him in the eye as the song rose to new heights. Diir raised his arms, staying connected to the crocodile only by virtue of his straining leg muscles. The elf twirled the short sword in his right hand so it pointed down, grasped the hilt in both fists, and raised the sword over his head. In one motion, Diir drove the point into the crocodile's brain.

The immediate effect on the crocodile devastated what remained of the span. The crocodile's massive tail slapped the wooden timbers into splinters. Water, smoke, and gore splashed around the leviathan's twisting body. The 30-foot reptile flung itself up onto its hind legs, thrashing and writhing. Bolts and arrows slammed into the monster's pale underbelly. Black gore welled up from the wounds.

The others had leaped clear as soon as Diir jammed the sword blade into the crocodile's head, and Devis, too, maneuvered to continue his ballad a little farther from the main action. The bard could not see what happened to Diir. He picked up the tempo on his lute and prayed for the haze to clear.

The upright crocodile snapped its head back like a whip, then the creature's body stiffened. Devis saw Diir fly into the air in a lazy arc that ended with a splash in the rushing waters of the Mormsilath. Devis squinted to see if Diir was floating or swimming, but could not spot the elf.

The crocodile stood improbably in midair for another full second. Devis thought he heard a keening, un-reptilian scream escape the crocodile's throat. The bard might also have seen a thin, blood red mist seep from the crocodile's empty eye sockets, but it could have been a trick of the smog and sunlight.

An involuntary, final twitch of the creature's tail, and the gigantic corpse belly flopped onto the southern bank of the river.

The bard wiped his eyes and scanned the river for Diir as he moved to help the others regain their feet. Takata was nowhere to be seen. Hound-Eye shouted her name with increasing urgency.

Devis spotted the quiet elf easily enough. The current held Diir pinned against the gore-splattered wreckage. The water level was rising rapidly against the elf's chest courtesy of the brand new dam formed by the fallen timbers and the crocodile's corpse.

Devis looked at his feet as cold water seeped into his boots, then back at Diir. The water bubbled against the struggling elf's face so that in a few seconds he'd be completely submerged. Devis caught Mialee's eye, but she shrugged—she had nothing that could help.

Pain creased the bard's side as he groped for his pack. He ignored it as his fingers closed around smooth metal and silk rope. He pulled the collapsible grappling hook over his head.

The hook was still collapsed, folded on clever hinges into a safe, rounded shape for easy packing. Devis's fingers fumbled with the device, trying to extend the prongs, then his eyes flicked over the water to check on Diir.

The peak of the elf's golden helm was all that broke the water's angry surface.

"Mialee! Magic?" he shouted.

"You want me to blast him? That's all I prepared for!" Mialee shouted back over the roar, stomping toward him.

"Takata! Takaaaaataaaaa!" Hound-Eye shouted.

Mialee snatched the silk rope and still folded hook without stopping. She twirled the metal over her head, then released the heavy weight. It splashed into the water with the rope across where Diir's body ought to be, if it had been above water.

Mialee pulled, but couldn't budge the rope. Her feet sank into the muddy bank and water swirled around her shins. Devis waded out to help her pull, hoping the rope wasn't snagged in the debris. It stretched taut, and Devis thanked Fharlanghn he'd bought the sturdy silk. The wetter it got, the tougher it got. Hemp might already have snapped against the raging current.

Through the tension in the rope, Devis felt small hands join his and Mialee's efforts a few feet behind. He glanced back, but still didn't see Takata, although Hound-Eye had stopped shouting for her. As Devis turned back to the river, something white flashed in his peripheral vision: a small, fur-covered boot at the end of a tiny, shattered leg protruding from beneath the crocodile's corpse. Devis understood the grim, horrified look in Hound-Eye's good orb as the tough little halfling hauled on the rope like an automaton. Hound-Eye, had found his wife. Now he was the last survivor of Tent City.

Takata was lost, but Diir could still be saved. The length of silk grudgingly began moving toward them. Four sets of arms hauled hand over hand. A few seconds later, Diir's face broke the surface with a loud gasp.

The soggy, exhausted band dragged themselves well clear of the Mormsilath's new course and flopped onto the road.

"Hound-Eye . . . sorry."

"Not your fault, bard," the gasping halfling replied. "She knew . . ."

"All the same . . . sorry. Bridge is out. Guess we're committed," Devis managed before blacking out.

Cavadrec popped Constable Muhn's last remaining eyeball into his mouth with a flick of a bony claw. The wight felt it pop between his teeth. He chewed deliberately as the fluid inside the morsel flooded his dry tongue.

He hadn't eaten this well in centuries. Animal eyes varied in quality and flavor, and Cavadrec found nothing was as sweet as the optic nerve of a sentient being. The halflings he'd discovered nesting in the Morkeryth ruins had been a nice appetizer—the first real feast of intelligent food he'd had since his confinement—but the dwarves' sizeable orbs made a much more satisfying meal.

The dwarves hadn't known what hit them, literally. As a wight, Cavadrec didn't necessarily need special magic to turn his enemies into minions, though that was his specialty. All he had to do was kill them personally. He'd relished the work, batting their useless weapons aside and pounding their faces into pulp with gnarled fists as one of them shouted curses at someone named Devis.

He made sure to pluck the delectable eyes while his victims still drew breath. Dead eyes, Cavadrec found, tasted simply awful. And his new wights could see well enough without them.

Cavadrec rolled the skin of Muhn's eyeball around his mouth and focused his concentration on the bridge. His second self, the semi-independent Cavadrec-mind that he'd sent to dominate the zombie crocodile, was finishing off Favrid's apprentice even as his wight-self enjoyed this repast. He felt a rush of physical power as his central awareness shifted from this skeletal form into the body of the massive crocodile. Again, he heard someone shout "Devis." Was this some local paladin? No, he saw through reptilian eyes, the Devis at the ruined bridge was plucking a ridiculous lute. The wight was reminded of his age-old defeat, in which a bard had played a part.

Through his crocodile eyes, he saw an elf wearing Silatham armor and clutching a silver blade yell and leap over the crocodilian snout. Cavadrec felt the weight of the warrior land solidly, and a pair of legs clamped around the back of his wide neck. Cavadrec's wight-body flinched involuntarily as the magical fire poured into the crocodile's flank from one side and arrows pierced its thick hide from the other.

One of the rangers had escaped the rats. Cavadrec was stunned. It was inconceivable that Favrid's young apprentice, the girl Mialee, could defeat the crocodile alone. Even half of the wight's power was more than enough to deal with the likes of her. But the elf woman had powerful allies. Cavadrec had not anticipated this development. Was the agile elf warrior the same one his wolves chased from Morkeryth? The dumb animals would not have recognized Silatham armor if they were wearing it.

Pain peppered his side and the bard's incessant singing rang painfully in his wrinkled, pointed, wight ears.

It was time to end this nonsense. Cavadrec began a prayer to Nerull, calling down a hideously powerful blast of necrotic energy that should not only destroy the elf woman and her allies, but the crocodile, the wreckage of the bridge, and most of the landscape for miles around. Cavadrec felt the complex spell building behind the crocodile's empty eye sockets as the legs around his neck tightened like a vise. Then the elf's blade split the crocodile's skull.

Miles away, Cavadrec the wight screamed.

He had been a wight for just under a thousand years, eight hundred more than he'd existed as a living elf. When he accepted the gift of Nerull soon after his imprisonment, he'd marveled at how his new wight body could tolerate harsh environments and most physical harm without the slightest discomfort. As an elf, he had been vulnerable. As a wight, he could endure the heat of the burning earth deep beneath Morsilath or a hail of arrows.

But in a thousand years of lurking beneath Morsilath, Cavadrec had never felt such pain.

His jagged talons dug into his own gray, leathery face and pulled strips of ragged skin from his skull. The wight dropped to his knees and screamed at the setting sun. Had any travelers been unfortunate enough to happen upon the scene, Cavadrec would have ripped them limb from limb. As it was, the wights he had just created, sensing weakness, surrounded their murderer.

He tore them apart instead, then turned and stalked back to the cracks in the rock face that led to his waiting mine cart.

The sun had been down for half an hour. Mialee scanned the forest for some sign of the wolves that hunted them. She wasn't just looking, she was magically scanning for their telltale, necrotic signatures. A few flickered black in her altered vision, but she had difficulty pinpointing individuals.

Hound-Eye, limping along beside her, cocked his good eye at the elf woman, who smiled and returned her gaze forward. "Scanning," she explained, "but it's hard to get a fix."

"Eight to the left, maybe a dozen to the right," Hound-Eye replied, "that I can see with one eye, anyway." He wasn't bothering to whisper. The hunters knew exactly where they were.

Twenty, at least. Mialee let her detection spell dissipate to conserve her energy. She had no reason to doubt Hound-Eye, which was odd, considering how they'd met. She found he was quite honest about his profession once she got to know him. If they were going to get to the bottom of this, the halfling said, he was coming along for the revenge, or would die trying to get it. He actually pulled up his eye patch, revealing an empty red socket, and swore to them by his good eye that he would not betray them.

The halfling claimed to know right where to find the "mythical" village of Silatham, and even now led them through the forest far from the overgrown wagon-track that ran to the ruins of Morkeryth and Tent City.

Devis patched up his own injuries with a little ditty, and the gnome cleric kept their most grievous wounds from bleeding out. Zalyn's ability as a healer was limited. The gnome did the best she could, but all were still hurting to some degree. They agreed, however, to save the last few healing potions in case of another battle. If the elf village really was nearby, they could get aid there.

The wolves started shadowing them shortly after the travelers moved away from the river. Diir informed them with unsmiling certainty that these wolves smelled familiar. Hound-Eye insisted this same pack had been part of the massacre at Tent City.

A dozen normal wolves would have been threatening, but Mialee was confident the group could handle such a threat. The creatures that Diir and Hound-Eye described were much more dangerous, akin to the crocodile: zombie-like creations displaying an unnerving amount of intelligence.

The wizard nearly asked Hound-Eye and Diir if they thought the creatures were herding them toward Silatham, but decided she didn't want to know. If she could see it, Diir and Hound-Eye were probably already aware of it.

Mialee's eyes flashed to Zalyn. The chatty gnome was silent. She had tried in vain to raise the halfling, Takata, but the prayers and invocations were beyond her. The failure seemed to have snuffed out part of her spirit.

Mialee nearly tripped on a tree root when Hound-Eye's gloved hand smacked her bare thigh. The halfling stopped and jerked a thumb over one shoulder.

"Slowly," he said, and turned. Mialee saw the others do the same from the corner of her eye.

Two black shapes loped along behind them through the trees, no longer making any pretense at lurking. Black pits stared soullessly at Mialee as one of the wolves raised its muzzle and let out a gurgling snarl. Three, four, six shapes fell in behind the first two, gaping jaws grinning with long yellow teeth. Eight behind them, picking up speed.

Everyone stopped. The wolves slowed and milled about with menace. A few seconds passed as hunters and hunted sized each other up. One of the zombie wolves uttered a low growl deep in its tattered throat, and the pack took up the same call.

Then the wolves roared and charged.

"Run!" shouted Devis, but they already were.

Driven by sheer survival instinct, the weary band barreled through the trees. Darji's raven-caw reached Devis's ears from high above. He glanced upward, but could not spot the raven against the moonless, black sky. The bird would no doubt catch up with them in Silatham, unless she beat them to it.

If he had wings, Devis would have been at the back rooms of the Silver Goblet by now. The bird had courage, but no appreciation for the finer things.

Devis knew stories about Silatham, of course. Any bard worth his lute strings knew the legendary local haunts. The village was certainly that. He'd never actually been there, however, and had never really believed Hound-Eye's insistent tales of mysterious rangers hunting halflings for meat. Diir's armor baffled the halfling, who swore the man was dressed like a "damned Silatham ranger." They'd had a difficult time convincing Hound-Eye that Diir wasn't going to betray them, but the quiet elf's obvious confusion about his own recent past persuaded the scruffy halfling to tolerate the ranger, if he was a ranger.

No one agreed on what the place was like—even Hound-Eye said he'd never actually been there, just "followed murderin' rangers until they disappeared, but I know where they disappeared and it's always the same place." According to myth and Hound-Eye's tales, the elves of Silatham were xenophobic in the extreme.

The bard gritted his teeth at the nagging pain in his side, which their limited medicine hadn't healed. Xenophobia he could handle. The elves, he was pretty sure, didn't want to eat him, and that alone would be a welcome change.

"I see a light!" Diir whispered. A dim orange glow resembling campfires ahead in the trees emerged as they crested a hillock. Zalyn picked up speed and passed the bard, leaving Devis trailing.

Devis squinted. He didn't see anything, damn his eyes.

"Don't make sense," Hound-Eye growled. "That's the spot all right, but there's never lights."

The bard marveled that the wolves had not attacked. The grinning, snarling, undead beasts yipped and barked like hyenas and were keeping pace easily. The things were playing with them like barn cats over a nest of mice.

Devis could think of only two reasons the wolves did not attack. Either they were simply trying to tire the prey out to the point where they couldn't fight back, or they were herding the group toward the rest of the pack. If Silatham was lost to the undead, so were he, Mialee, and the rest.

The bard heard a rasping growl behind him and risked a glance over his shoulder. The lead zombie wolf was literally snapping at his heels. Devis pulled his long sword free of its scabbard and slashed awkwardly behind his back as he ran. He felt the blade tip make brief, fleshy contact. The wolf yelped and fell back. The sword was clumsy to hold while running, but he held onto it in case another wolf tried the same trick.

Devis lifted his gaze from his friends' running backsides—how had he been chosen to bring up the rear?—and thought he could finally make out a faint light ahead. Dozens of bloody paws crashed through the brush behind them on the overgrown trail. He hoped the elves were ready for a fight. The bard and his allies were bringing a doozy to their front door. Unless, of course, they were running right into the talons of even more undead creatures.

Devis didn't need the eyes of a full-blooded elf to see the bright flash of blue light ahead of them on the dark forest trail. A lone elf stood in the road about two hundred feet away, facing away from them. The elf was tall, thin, and wore tattered robes that hung from his lanky frame. Atop the elf's head was a pointed, silver helm. Devis could make out no further details. Normally, even his half-human eyes should have been able to see the buttons on the man's coat at this distance, but the moons were down and the only other sources of light were the distant orange glow and the pale light spell Zalyn had asked Mialee to cast on her helm.

Devis heard the wolves snarling and yapping behind them. For whatever reason, the creatures were staying back. The bard hoped that meant they were afraid of the tall man. Maybe he was just an elf.

Mialee gasped. "Favrid?" the elf woman whispered.

"Favrid?" the others responded simultaneously.

"It could be," the elf woman hissed. "Teleportation is no big feat for him."

"Why didn't he teleport himself to safety?" Devis whispered as the group maneuvered to keep watch on the wolves and the shadowy figure. "Why won't he face you? I don't trust it, love."

"Why doesn't he do something?" Zalyn asked.

"Because he's a wizard, that's why," Hound-Eye spat. "He didn't save Tent City, did he?"

Darji circled low over their heads. "Hound-Eye, Favrid did everything he could," the little raven chirped.

"I'll tell that to the dead, when I get a chance to bury them," the halfling retorted darkly.

"Favrid!" Mialee shouted. "Master, I've come to help!"

"What?" Devis said as Mialee ran ahead. "Mialee, wait!"

The solitary figure did not turn. Another wolf howled, and the stinking pack drew closer.

"Planes!" Devis swore and jogged ahead to keep up with her. She was fast.

"Mialee."

The voice that spoke the elf woman's name drifted down the road through the cool night air from the direction of the lanky figure. It reminded Devis of pipe-smoking old Gunnivan. The voice was gravelly and deep, but had the mellifluous quality of a practiced stage performer or epic balladeer.

The party collectively stopped, Mialee far ahead, Devis behind, and the others watching them, the tall man, and the wolves. The wolves howled mournfully and whimpered.

"Favrid," Mialee said breathlessly. "I'm here. We're coming to help."

"My child, I'm injured," the voice intoned paternally, but with a hint of urgency.

Mialee again broke into a run toward the figure, stumbled, recovered. "He needs help!" Mialee yelled over her shoulder.

Devis and the others dashed to follow.

"Mialee, I don't think—" Devis shouted, but broke off to bat at a snapping snout near his heel. A knot gripped his belly. Something about this smelled bad, and it wasn't just zombie wolves and crocodile guts.

Mialee could not believe her good luck. Her heart leaped in her chest. The last few days had lasted for decades. Now, after all her searching, the miles and miles of terrified running, she was about to reunite with her old teacher and find sanctuary. The old man would have little trouble dealing with the monsters yapping at their heels. Devis may not have been able to see the old elf clearly at a distance, but Mialee could make out every line and garish color as soon as the blue flash of teleportation had subsided around the distant figure.

She heard a caw above and wondered why Darji wasn't on Favrid's shoulder already. The bird would certainly confirm what Mialee already felt in her heart. Her old teacher, whom she now realized she had missed terribly, was alive, and hurt.

The wizard heard the snarling wolves and the pounding of booted feet as her enemies and allies alike tried to keep up. The trail ahead broke into a clearing where Favrid stood, with a wall of thick trees beyond. Gentle sounds slid through her mind like the memory of a dream.

"Mialee," the warm, familiar voice drifted to her ears, "hurry, Mialee."

The voice pulled her insistently away from her companions. The elf woman ignored the pain in her legs and increased her lead ahead of Diir, Devis, Zalyn, and Hound-Eye.

She was so close. Favrid still faced away from Mialee, but she would have recognized the garish robes and aged hunch anywhere. Long, white strands of thinning hair flowed down the old elf's back. Favrid had lost the hair on top of his head at the tender age of 80, but insisted on trimming the wispy locks that remained only under extreme duress.

The silver, pointed helm was unfamiliar to her and looked somewhat out of place, but she could only imagine the dangers Favrid had faced since he'd sent Darji to find her. The helm looked well used and bore many dents and nicks, no doubt souvenirs of Favrid's miraculous escape.

Darji. Where was she?

She knows I am here, a gentle voice whispered in Mialee's skull.

Of course. The little bird must already feel Favrid. Even now the raven must be communicating with him from some lofty vantage point overhead. The old wizard had not yet turned to face her because he was concentrating on the contact. It had to be Favrid. The powerful wizard would protect them and destroy the foul predators that threatened to devour her. As she drew close to her former master, her heart swelled with certainty and warmth. She reached an open hand out and placed it on Favrid's shoulder.

Beneath Mialee's fingertips, Favrid's robes disintegrated, becoming torn, ragged purple tatters. Patches of leathery gray skin showed through the tattered clothing. Sliver-white strands of soft, elven hair twisted into coiled black wire. Mialee felt pain and put a finger to her temple. Her friends pounded down the road behind, suddenly screaming. Devis shouted something she didn't understand. Favrid's head and shoulders swiveled as the old man turned to face the elf woman at last.

Red, pinpoint eyes flashed in black sockets. The wight's hand shot out and grasped Mialee around the throat. His grinning, toothy rictus leaked black blood as the creature hissed fetid air into Mialee's face.

"Mialee," the creature rasped as its lips twisted into a leer, and the wizard girl saw a black tongue that looked like a slug roll sickeningly in the wight's mouth. The creature's bony skull cocked to the right. It raised one wrinkled eyebrow as it added with false pathos, "Hurry."

This, Mialee thought with sudden clarity, was not Favrid. The gnarled fist around her neck squeezed tighter. Mialee felt her toes leave the ground as the wight lifted her to look her in the eye.

Mialee couldn't breathe and her head was filling with fog. The smell of the thing was overwhelming. Had she not been wearing the athel wood collar, she would have been dead already, and even the resilient wood could not protect her for long. Her arms flailed at her waist for a knife or a wand, Zalyn's trail rations, anything she could use as a weapon against the wight. Her hands, numb and tingling, could not grasp anything.

"Drop the girl and back away!" a welcome voice boomed theatrically behind Mialee.

She was in no position to see, but she heard two crossbows lock as the bard and Zalyn slid bolts into place. She heard Diir's short sword clear its scabbard and Hound-Eye's arrow slip from its quiver into the short bow.

Mialee's vision was turning red, and a sound like ocean surf became a dull roar in her ears. From the corner of her eye, she saw lupine shadows circling them like sharks. How polite of them, she mused deliriously.

The wight holding Mialee snapped his head back and cackled into the sky. "I don't think so," the wight hissed.

"All right," Devis's voice echoed distantly, bravely, she thought deliriously, "but we asked nicely."

The twang of bowstrings pierced the ocean roar in Mialee's ears. She forced her sleepy eyes to open and saw that her attacker now boasted an arrow in its chest and a crossbow bolt in either shoulder. The monster didn't flinch, but plucked the arrow from its chest while keeping Mialee in the air with the other hand. She kicked weakly at the creature, which held up the arrow and examined it.

"Halflings," the creature snarled at the arrow in its claws. "Tasty, tasty halflings."

The wight dropped the arrow and opened its jaws to the sky. It snarled, barked, and howled like a mad wolf, and the circling predators yelped in reply.

The last voice Mialee heard was Devis's.

"Does anyone have another plan?" the half-elf asked.

Then she was flying through the air, something hard struck her skull, icy pain sliced her neck, and she died.

Devis, his lute forgotten and his crossbow on the trail behind, swung his sword blade madly into the snarling wolves. The wolves kept him from reaching her, and now the thing had her by the throat. Devis furiously hacked at ruined muzzles and torn hides, fighting his way through the pack with a fury he hadn't known dwelled inside him. He drove his sword through a hairy skull, heard a whimper, and charged to the helpless elf woman's aid.

He was still several agonizing feet away when the wight tossed Mialee aside with a casual flick of its bony hand. Devis froze. He had been so close.

The elf woman smashed headfirst against the base of a huge, old tree and Devis heard the sickening snap of vertebrae. She did not move and didn't seem to be breathing. Her limbs splayed awkwardly, her head twisted at an angle that no living person could accommodate without excruciating pain. Glassy eyes stared into the trees above, unblinking, unmoving.

Mialee was dead.

Blind fury surged through Devis's body.

Mialee was dead.

He screamed and charged the wight. Only rage guided his sword. He would cut this monster into a thousand pieces, burn the body, and drop the foul ashes into the dead crater of Morsilath itself. The silver blade sliced the air.

Mialee was dead.

A black staff appeared from nowhere in the wight's hands. The bard's sword hit the ebony wood and bounced back. Devis bellowed and maneuvered to strike again. The wight twirled the staff in both hands like a fighting monk.

Heavy black wood, hard as deknae, cracked across Devis's jaw. The bard flipped painfully onto his back. The sword slipped from his hand. His eyes rolled to his right, and he saw the blade embedded point-first in the hard earth, hilt waving in mock greeting.

Devis clambered back to his feet and yanked the sword free from the earth. The snarling wolf pack circled more distantly now, waiting to snap up anyone who ran from the fight. Diir circled and flanked the wight opposite Devis, dodging blows from the creature's black staff. Zalyn shouted a battle cry and charged into the fray in her gleaming armor, and the wight promptly sent her flying with the butt of the staff. She landed with a clang, but couldn't get up in the awkward armor.

Devis glanced around for Hound-Eye. The halfling had abandoned them after all. Devis would kill him. Then he spotted Hound-Eye crouched over the fallen elf woman, trying to get her to swallow a potion from Zalyn's leather bag. The bard detected no movement in Mialee's limp body, even after Hound-Eye tossed an empty vial over his shoulder, cursing and shaking Mialee gently. Potions could only do so much.

Revenge was a simple, animal thing, but Devis wanted it more than anything. He forced himself to turn away from Mialee's lifeless eyes and face her killer.

He should have stopped her. Why hadn't she listened when he warned her? It had to be magic. He should have caught up to the elf woman and held her back. He should have stood beside her and faced down Muhn and his guards, then taken the elf woman far away.

He should have stopped her.

He held no hope that they'd be able to find anyone powerful enough to bring her back from the beyond. Silatham was no good, he knew with chilling certainty. The "lost outpost" had not, apparently, been able to stop the undead. He knew Zalyn couldn't do it, and the missing brothers of her order were dead and stumbling around Silatham without eyes even now, if they'd gotten that far.

Devis ducked back from the wight's staff as it cut the air in front of his face. Focus, bard. He brought up his sword blade and felt it block the staff and violently bounce back.

The bard redirected his attack and sliced his sword into the creature's leg. The wight screeched and shoved the base of the black staff into Diir's gut. The elf retched and doubled over onto all fours. His swords clattered on either side of him.

Devis took advantage of the wight's distraction with expert timing. His long sword sliced the air and carved a neat arc through the back of the wight's neck, though the cut did not decapitate the creature. Before he could try again, one gray fist flew up from the creature and connected with a loud crack against his chin. The bard staggered to his knees.

Diir's short sword lay next to Devis's boots. He saw Diir struggling on the ground, coughing up blood as the wight turned from Devis and moved to strike the ranger again.

Devis dropped his own weapon and took up the blade Diir used to kill the crocodile.

The wight turned and loomed over the stunned Diir, who seemed unable to focus on the monster inches away. Hound-Eye wailed at the gods while Zalyn kicked and squirmed like an over-turned beetle. Devis heard no sound from Mialee.

Devis raised the short sword behind his head and took two quick breaths. His eyes narrowed at the tattered rags that hung from the thing's gray, leathery back, and he hurled the short sword end over end like a carnival performer.

The throw was going to miss. The weapon tumbled away from him as time crawled to a standstill.

In the split second that was available, Devis managed to sing a single line that summoned a glowing hand-shape beside the tumbling sword. With it, he nudged the blade toward the wight. If he'd miscalculated the weight of the unfamiliar sword, it would simply smack against the monster like a club. In the process, they would lose what was probably the most powerful weapon they had.

Devis calculated correctly. The tip of the silver sword pierced the wight's back squarely between its hunched shoulder blades. The heavy blade sunk in to the hilt. The skeletal thing screeched in agony, and Devis smiled bitterly.

The black staff fell by the wayside as the wight clawed at the silver weapon. The hilt protruded from its back while the tip, extending several inches from the creature's chest, gleamed dully in the starlight. Devis stalked forward empty-handed, fists clenched, the last man standing. He grasped the sword and kicked hard at the creature's back. It stumbled forward onto its belly, then clawed and writhed on the bare ground. The thing was dreadfully hurt, yet it seethed with power.

As Diir regained his senses, he crab-crawled away from the thrashing flurry of rags and limbs nearby.

Then the wight's red eyes locked onto the short sword in Devis's hand. A vile curse exploded from it in a language the bard barely comprehended. Pinpricks of scarlet light deep in black sockets flashed intensely. Were they focused on Devis, the sword, or both?

Devis edged closer to the creature, which was now on all fours and trying to stand. A bony arm extended toward the fallen staff.

The slash across the back of the wight's neck formed a fleshy, ridiculous smile. If the sword could hurt the wight, Devis was willing to gamble that it could take the thing's head right off with little difficulty. He raised the magical blade overhead.

Before he could strike, the pinpricks of red in the wight's eye sockets flared brightly and the monster snarled a string of unintelligible invective. The air around it rippled like a heat mirage, and it disappeared.

The short sword cut through empty air. Devis lost his balance and barely caught himself before tumbling again to the ground. He blinked and looked at the short sword clutched in his hand, not quite sure what had just happened. Had the wight disintegrated, or disappeared? Was it gone or still here, invisible? Devis scanned the surrounding darkness.

A faint orange glow still flickered in the distance. The wolves had scattered, though he knew not why. Devis decided the wight, too, was gone. He dropped the short sword and ran to Mialee with a black knot of dread twisting in his belly.

Hound-Eye looked up into the bard's eyes. His face was wet with tears, and he convulsed with choking sobs.

"I'm sorry," the halfling choked, "I used all of our potions. They're no good!"

Devis gazed down at the glass-eyed, still-beautiful elf woman and felt tears crawling down his cheeks. Hound-Eye was right. Mialee's neck was broken.

"*Ehlonna hinue, Mormhaor shan!*"

Zalyn was on her feet and conjuring something to pursue the fleeing wolves and keep them running. Were his attention not consumed by the dead woman before him, Devis might have been surprised that their inexperienced young cleric had suddenly found the wherewithal to repel two dozen undead wolves. He might have noticed that the god the little cleric invoked was not the Protector. If Devis's eyes had not been glued to Mialee's body, he might even have spied the gnome tucking a golden icon engraved with a tree and unicorn into her leather bag.

Devis knelt and closed the girl's dead eyes with the backs of his fingertips, the only part of his hands not covered in wight gore. He noted sadly that Mialee's soft, pale skin did not flinch when an errant tear freed itself from his face and landed on her cheek.

A tiny gauntlet fell on his shoulder. "The brothers . . . they can—" Zalyn began.

The brothers from her temple. Devis, in his fury and grief, had not believed it possible they were alive. But even if the chance was slim, he had to try. He took his abandoned long sword from Diir and sheathed it.

Devis scooped the woman's body into his arms and stood. The rage gave way to resolve and a glimmer of hope. Still, their little band was so beaten and battered.

"Zalyn," he said, "I think the odds . . . they're not good. That thing was waiting for her."

"There is at least one cleric of the Protector in Silatham capable of bringing her back, Devis," Zalyn said, and her impish voice became heavy with an authority Devis had never heard from the little gnome before. "I feel it in my heart," the gnome added, pounding a gauntlet into her armored chest.

"Let's go find your cleric. He'd better be alive, because he's going to help her, or I'll kill him."

Cavadrec hurled the teleportation helm with all his considerable supernatural might at the black deknae throne that dominated his underground lair. The metal clanged loudly off the heat-treated stone and bounced against the flank of a surprised zombie wolf before finally settling onto the floor, mocking him. Favrid's head lolled to one side, and the battered, old elf cracked a smile despite the agony Cavadrec knew he felt. Cavadrec considered killing the fool on the spot, but restrained himself. Such an impulsive act, satisfying in the short term, would be disastrous for his ultimate plan. Instead, he decided to crush the old man's spirit.

"Your idiot girl is dead, old friend," the wight hissed into Favrid's face. "I killed her myself."

He drove a fist into the old wizard's gut for emphasis. Favrid coughed up something black that dribbled down the front of his pale, bare chest.

Favrid groaned. Cavadrec welcomed the anguished sound. His mood improved slightly. He should have brought the old fool down here ages ago.

The wolf dashed off down one of the many exits that led from Cavadrec's lair into the maze of lava tubes crisscrossing the earth beneath Morsilath and the surrounding forest.

Cavadrec reflected on the battle that had cost the apprentice her useless life. The wight seethed.

So the blade had been recovered. The pain it inflicted was great, but the bard had caught him off guard. If the wight faced the blade again, it would be on his terms. He knew all about Favrid and Linnelle and their little plan, although Linnelle had not lived to see it come to fruition. Favrid would, but not as the old man expected. Cavadrec had removed the wizard from the equation personally. With the elf woman out of the way and the ridiculous gnome their only divine hope, they would never escape Silatham alive. All that remained was to alert the troops.

While Favrid whimpered and moaned in the dimly lit cave, Cavadrec focused his consciousness on one of his most useful servants.

His wight-self cracked into a death's head grin at what he saw when he looked out through the tiny, borrowed eye sockets of the wightling rat.

The remaining members of the party walked wearily onward toward the mysterious glow of Silatham. Despite the sad burden he carried, Devis gaped when he saw the place.

A curved wall of wood, woven together with ancient elven techniques like Dogmar's strange Temple of the Protector, rose into the massive evergreen trees and disappeared into the darkness high above. The massive trunks of the old-growth forest of Silath were embedded into the wall, or more likely the wall had been grown around them.

Silatham looked like an enormous, splayed onion impaled on huge evergreen trees. Several rope ladders hung down over the ground, and a curved leaf of the onion—maybe an artichoke—opened out to form a ramp that could support heavy weight; carts, horses, even marching troops. That explained the clearing. It was a mustering or unloading area. Drop your big artichoke ramp, load it up with soldiers, and the elevation renders them well-defended, Devis thought.

Of course, the place was on trees. Fire could be a problem for defenders. Live athel trees were impervious to most natural flame, and the trees had no doubt been soaked with defensive magic. The problem with this bustling town scenario—in addition to the fact that it was a myth—was location, location, location. Devis couldn't understand how this place would support itself. It sat ringed by dense forest that would break a pack mule's leg in a minute. It wasn't large enough to have farms inside the onion wall. And you'd have to haul soil up a hundred feet to grow anything in treetop gardens.

This could only mean one thing. There had to be huge stores of food under this place: steaks, bread, wine, and ale. It all had to have been brought in before the trees grew up to surround it. Silatham had been stuck up there when this forest was very, very young.

Which meant that the huge, central tree sticking up through the onion had to be a fake. It was as big as the rest, but it had to be the route to the stores. Devis was suddenly very hungry. He shifted Mialee on his hip, and her arm flopped free and struck Hound-Eye. The little halfling yelped and moved ahead of the bard.

Devis's arms ached. It was time to give up on the romantic hero bit for a moment. He flung Mialee over his left shoulder and jogged to catch up with Hound-Eye and the others. He winced every time he heard the lute smack her in the head and decided to just walk fast. Diir was already starting up one of the rope ladders. Devis hoped the ranger knew a secret way in.

The elf seemed to know where he was going, and that was encouraging. Devis still didn't trust the glow. The splayed onion looked as if someone had lit a candle inside. This place wasn't all dark, living athel. It was dead, and burning. Devis could actually feel the heat on his face.

From close up, Devis could see gaps, open seams where the woven wood had dried and split from age. This was dead athel like the temple in Dogmar, not dark, living trees.

Devis knew a surprising amount about athel trees, learned from a big-eared elven artisan in exchange for a tune and a good word with a barmaid at the Dog's Ear. The thing about athel wood was, it could grow in the ground—like the temple once had—or on other trees. Elves used to use the stuff to build in the trees before athel became so rare. When it was alive, athel trees could be woven using a technique very similar to bardic magic and it was dark, rich, reddish brown. When athel died, it turned golden yellow like the temple, or white, if not treated properly.

The tops of the dead, woven athel trees of Silatham spread up and out like the petals of a huge blossom, in a shape the elves called *ama*, "flower." It still looked like an onion to Devis.

The curved platforms were known as *xilos*, or petals. The xilos formed wide platforms that held what looked like lookout stations. Such a vantage point would be extremely effective in the town's defense, Devis figured, since one could literally get the drop on any enemy charging the wall while staying out of that enemy's reach. As long as the athel resisted the most obvious angle of attack on the outpost, it could stand unmolested for millennia. Which, he guessed, it had. According to what the wrinkled, little letch at the Dog's Ear had said, athel wood could also be coaxed with magic to close the enormous flower petals in a truly heavy siege, creating a spiked, straight wall twice as tall as the "open artichoke" design he gazed at.

The others had all followed Diir up the rope ladder. Only the bard with the dead elf woman over one shoulder still stood gaping at Silatham.

With Mialee's body tied awkwardly to his back, Devis heaved himself and his precious cargo belly-first onto the xilo, keeping the elf woman's lifeless head from cracking against the living wood. Zalyn helped him ease the burden onto the hard surface of the wide lookout spot. He rolled into a crouch and peered over the elven village of Silatham.

The place was a wreck. At least, Devis assumed the inhabitants would think so. In truth, the place was so strange looking to the city-bred bard that he couldn't have said for certain whether it was in ruins or in perfect condition. But he was willing to bet the elves didn't normally burn house-sized fires in their residences just to keep warm, athel wood or no athel wood. The old trees that grew up through the base of the onion were covered in white athel houses that glowed with reflected firelight. Devis wonderd how long it would be before the whole place went up. Even dead, the wood looked to be resisting the flames. Most of what burned, he saw as he looked closer, were the Silath tree support structures, not athel, which just smoldered instead.

He soon spied one athel structure that was unmistakably important, the tallest in the village. Devis guessed that it led to storerooms of food, weapons, maybe even riches. No symbol adorned the outside of the structure, but Devis could feel the holiness of the tall, peaked building. It must have been a temple, and that was exactly what Mialee needed. High up the sides of the central Silath tree, which was no doubt dead athel stained brown, a few cozy residences or study rooms perched above the rest of the village.

Only after adjusting to the alien architecture did Devis realize that what he thought were rustling branches and drifting leaves were actually thousands of undead elves. They shambled about the bases of the trees, unseeing, uncaring, unaware of their condition.

The only structure that any of them were climbing was the temple tree at the center of the village. Dead elves climbed like rats up the rope ladders strung around the temple. Why they didn't go inside, Devis didn't know. Maybe that cleric Zalyn placed so much trust in actually was here and was somehow keeping the dead at bay.

Zalyn moved very slowly toward Devis to avoid making noise in what was left of her full battle dress, and the bard was impressed with the gnome's success. She had left all but the breastplate on the ground outside Silatham, wrapped in her cloak and stuffed behind a tree. The sacrifice would help them sneak into the place. Zalyn approached Mialee and crouched over the wizard's lifeless body. Devis left her alone with her rites, or whatever they were. Despite the destruction, there really seemed to be cause for hope. Mialee would be her old self again in no time, Devis was positive.

They had to get inside that central tree, Devis thought. That would mean getting past the zombies shuffling among the ruins and clinging to the rope ladders. If only Mialee weren't dead. He contemplated the big temple tree. Not every ladder had zombies on it, a few were clear. If he could get to an open ladder with Mialee ...

... the weight of an adult elf tied to his back would get him killed and both of them devoured, or worse. Maybe Zalyn could turn enough of the things to clear a swath. Diir could help, too, if this really was his town.

Diir tapped the bard on the shoulder and pointed to their right at another xilo lookout. Devis saw a lithe figure, so still the half-elf had missed it before. The silent shape seemed to be watching the village below and the shuffling things that infested it. The bard had difficulty seeing the figure's face through the haze. Diir pointed out the shape to Hound-Eye and Zalyn. The foursome collectively squinted at the figure for a sign of movement.

The crouching form remained so completely motionless it could have been a stone gargoyle. It was, however, covered in pale armor that looked curiously familiar to the bard.

As he caught a glimpse of Diir from the corner of his eye, Devis nearly smacked himself on the forehead. The motionless figure was wearing the same peculiar style of armor as the taciturn elf. In fact, Diir perched on their xilo in a posture that was the mirror image of their crouching observer.

The bard could only believe that the figure was enjoying the show below. Or, he admitted grudgingly, it was an elf just like Diir, maybe with the same memory loss and only a homeward-turning compulsion to return to this place.

The four of them communicated through hushed whispers and gestures, and settled on trying to reach the figure, which still had not moved. If it turned out to be friendly, and it had a sword like Diir's, their chances for success would improve dramatically.

Unfortunately, Devis knew they were kidding themselves. It was ridiculous to assume weapons like that grew on trees, even in a place where houses did. If everyone in this place had a Diir-sword, Silatham wouldn't be burning. But still, the distant, crouching elf—please, the bard thought, let him be an elf, if he turns into a wight in front of my eyes I'm just going to jump to my death—was their best hope of figuring out what had happened to the village. Even with normal weapons, if the man was half the fighter Diir had proven himself to be, he would be a valuable ally.

The party silently elected Devis to approach the crouching figure. Hound-Eye would once have been a better choice, but his lame foot would be a liability now. Zalyn and Diir had to stay behind. The elf and that magic sword of his were the group's best hope for survival if Devis didn't make it back. The bard wasn't keen on leaving Mialee's body behind, but Zalyn assured him through hand signals that she would see nothing disturbed the dead girl. He spared Mialee's lifeless face one last glance and flipped a wave to the others, then set off over the xilo toward the still-unmoving figure.

To reach the xilo, he had to climb along the narrow, upraised lip of a drawbridge ramp. He hugged the wood as wind and heat caused the ramp to sway back and forth in its locks.

A shift in the breeze sent heat and smoke washing over him when he was halfway across. Lungs stinging, eyes streaming, the bard crawled blindly on. Devis felt the end of the drawbridge, then his right hand pressed down on something soft. The something squeaked. He squeezed his eyes open against the particle-filled air and saw that his hand rested on a rat. A dead rat, from the look of it. The thing had no eyes.

Yet it squirmed under his gloved palm and Devis saw that it was trying desperately to twist its tiny head around to bite him. Not dead—undead. The little zombie squeaked, and the squeek became a screech.

Devis did the first thing that popped into his head. He smashed the furry rat's body with his fist. With a pop, foul-smelling gore, fur, and flesh burst from the creature. Devis marveled at how much awful stuff had been inside the little body. His nose flared in disgust and he let the rat corpse drop to the ground.

Devis was nearly to the crouching man. The smoke was so thick that Devis couldn't see the man's position, however, and he decided that the smoke would conceal him just as well. After pulling himself off the ramp, he crouched and walked carefully through the haze to a point near where the elf should be, if it was indeed an elf.

The wind shifted and the smoke cleared. The crouching man was gone. Devis rocked onto his knees to look all around just as something heavy struck him across the back of the skull.

18

Mialee dreamed of eternity.

The energy that was the essence of the wizard no longer thought of herself in terms of a name. She had no name, but she did have vague memories of words. Some words were names, such as "Mialee," "Biksel," "Favrid," and something called a "Devis."

Really, Mialee did not "think" at all in the conventional sense. Thoughts did not move through a brain of tissue and blood, crackling electrically from nerve to nerve. Instead, she existed because she knew she existed. She was energy and vague consciousness. What had been the essence of Mialee the wizard soared through the multiverse, propelled across planes of existence by nothing more than will to move. It orbited distant, blue suns in a heartbeat, stopped in on the end of time. More words resurfaced: "spellbook," "notes," "stars." There was both surprise and delight that stars were not just points of light, but immense beyond imagining.

And there was something else. Memories, perhaps, or hints of memories, of a physical world, one among millions. Why was there memory here? This was no place for memory. What was happening?

What could happen to conscious energy?

Another memory intruded. It hinted at life and afterlife, spirits and souls. Was this afterlife? After-what-life? Suddenly, the consciousness wanted very much to be somewhere else. The limitless expanse of the roiling multiverse was on fire . . .

A hand clasped her ankle. Such a strange sensation, yet comfortable.

A voice carried over the tumultuous ether. The sound echoed in the flaming void.

"Mialee," the voice whispered, shouted, and sang.

"What?" Mialee asked.

$\gg\!\!\!\ll$

Mialee's eyes blinked open.

She found herself looking up at the beaming faces of Zalyn and Devis. A tiny raven perched on the cleric's shoulder. Darji squawked in surprise. "She's awake!"

Hound-Eye and Diir also stood over her, wearing looks of relief. A stranger, a male elf adorned with the same antique armor that Diir wore, also loomed. This newcomer looked as if he'd seen even more combat than Diir. She felt warmth and heard the crackle of a fire in a fireplace, and past the onlookers she could see a high, curved ceiling of smooth, brown wood. The height was misleading because of her prone position. Her eyes rolled left and right and she saw that the room was fairly cramped. It held another couple of strangers and . . . a child? She smelled incense, tea leaves, and something else, something foul.

The nasty smell was coming from her clothes, which still pinched like a corset. And Devis. And Diir. All of them were covered in—

The events of the last few days came back in a rush, and Mialee bolted upright, eyes wide. She stared at Devis and squinted.

"Snowdrop?" Mialee asked. "Pear best tax collector green?"

The others stared at her. All but Devis and Zalyn actually took a step back.

Mialee frowned. What was going on?

"Snowdrop!" the girl barked. Slowly and loudly, like an aristocrat trying to explain an order to a dim servant, she repeated her question. "Pear . . . best . . . tax collector . . . green? Sextant owl?"

"Zalyn," the bard said, worried, "What's she saying? What did you do?"

"Um," Zalyn explained, "I resurrected her. The most powerful resurrection spell I know. Ehlonna should have returned her to perfect health." The gnome shrugged. "Maybe it had something to do with the broken ne—I mean, many scholars believe the voice comes from—" She shook her head and pursed her lips. "This isn't a normal side effect, I swear."

"What in blazes is a 'sextant owl'?" Hound-Eye asked.

"Troll interrogate sickle, snowdrop," Mialee said more urgently in an effort to get Devis to explain what was going on. "Goblin trampoline bugbear!"

They all just blinked. Mialee fumed.

"Oh, dear," the little gnome muttered, and she dashed off to her large leather satchel. She rummaged through the clanking vials and produced an empty one, then held it up in the firelight to read a tiny label that Mialee could hardly see. The elf wearing armor like Diir's looked at the label over her shoulder.

"What is it, elder?" said the elf.

"Haystack?" Mialee asked in shock. Zalyn didn't look like an "elder." She was barely an adult gnome.

"Yes, that's it," Zalyn said and pursed her lips at Mialee. "Aphasia."

"Marmot proclivity?" Mialee replied. When she received another round of blank stares, she leaped off the wooden table and jabbed an index finger at the vial. "Friendship! Apple friendship!" she repeated, exasperated.

Zalyn looked apologetic. "Mialee, I'm sorry. When you died —"

"Pear turnip swimming?" Mialee asked. She died? She remembered everything up until the point she spotted Favrid down the forest trail, then nothing.

Hound-Eye jumped in. "When the thing, er, killed you, I sort of panicked," the halfling explained sheepishly. Mialee guessed the man didn't often confess panicking. "I took a bunch of those potions and poured them into your mouth."

"It seems one of them wasn't a healing potion, though," Zalyn interrupted. "It was something we call *hinual quar*, the 'talking dance.' I assure you, I had no idea the brothers kept this sort of thing in their stock. Probably left there by someone trying to play a joke."

There was something changed about the gnome's voice. She spoke with confidence, authority, and no trace of the nasal accent of the Dogmar gutters. Zalyn frowned and continued her explanation.

"It's a prank potion, really, popular with youngsters and students. They think it humorous to slip it into the teacher's tea before lectures, that sort of thing." The gnome shrugged apologetically. "I believe that we've inadvertently given you aphasia, Mialee. The effect is temporary, I assure you."

"Dragon turtle dangle?" Mialee asked.

"Can she hear herself?" Devis asked the gnome. "Does she know what she's saying?"

"Turnip gazebo wagon, potato," Mialee told him.

"I do not believe so," Zalyn replied, "I suspect that she has every belief that the words leaving her lips are perfectly clear."

Mialee began to say something more, but snapped her mouth shut. It would explain the situation. She didn't remember swallowing any potions, though, let alone dying.

The creature had her by the throat, but her athel wood collar protected her from the wight's crushing strength. . . .

Sweet Ehlonna. Her final memory, walled off by the resurrection spell to keep her from losing her mind when she returned to life. The feeling of brief flight followed by a crunch, and agonizing pain followed by a split-second of chilling numbness before life left her body. The wight had killed her. She'd seen light and colors, dimly remembered. All of which made her presence in this cramped room all the more baffling. Zalyn certainly could not have brought her back from the dead—the little gnome was barely a novice, and not even accepted into her order, despite what she'd said. That was just lunacy.

"Will it pass?" asked Devis.

Mialee nodded agreement for the question, trying not to baffle anyone further.

"Certainly," Zalyn offered, "but without knowing how large a dose she received, I cannot say how long it will take. There must have still been some of the potion in her mouth when Ehlonna granted me the power to bring her back from the beyond. Perhaps it was a half dose, a quarter dose, or—"

"Or maybe we're stuck with a wizard who can't cast spells," Hound-Eye growled. "I don't know if any of you have noticed, but we need her."

Mialee regarded the halfling with an arched brow.

Hound-Eye blushed, scowled, and added, "Well, don't we? We need the girl to fight those things. I never heard a mage burn a zombie with 'turnip wagon potato'."

Turning from the discussion, Mialee listened closely to the sounds outside and thought she heard low voices—no clear words, but a cacophony of moans, groans, and guttural growls. Mialee noted for the first time that the few windows in the small room were boarded up, in a hurry from the look of it. The sounds she heard were not all animals. A low chorus of moaning, rasping voices growled in mockery of the lilting sounds of elves. These were elves with nothing to say but "urrrrrrrrrrrrrr."

Mialee placed a hand on the wand and felt her fingertips brush the comforting weight of her spellbook. She slapped her forehead. Of course! She couldn't' speak, but she might not be illiterate. But the special pages of the spellbook were made for spells. To scribble notes to her friends in it would be a terrible waste. She waved her hands at the others. With frantic gestures, she indicated she needed something to write on, and pulled out her dipless quill from the book pouch.

"I think she wants parchment," Diir said.

"There must be something, Soveliss," the other armored elf said, and moved to rummage through a desk that was pushed against a second door.

Mialee took the time then to peer at the other occupants of the room who had not yet said a word. One, a bald, scholarly elf in expensive-looking but gore-spattered robes, huddled next to the fire and regarded everyone with nervous eyes. Crouched beside him was an elf woman holding a very young elf child—perhaps no older than seven years—on her hip. The family, for that's exactly what they appeared to be, was less filthy than everyone else present, including Mialee, but still looked like they'd been through hell. These people were terrified and in no mood for conversation. The bald man looked like he trusted no one and meant to keep his family as far from the others as he could in the tiny space.

"Banana?" she asked, pointing at Diir.

As she was beginning to expect, the others were baffled. She walked to Diir and positioned herself between her ally and the other elf. She jabbed her finger at the man rummaging through the desk while she flapped her other hand like a bird beak next to her mouth. "Ba. Na. Na."

"I think she wants to know why Clayn referred to me as 'Soveliss'," Diir jumped in. Mialee marveled at his wordiness. "Elder," Diir said to Zalyn, "perhaps you could explain?"

Mialee sighed. Everyone she knew had gone insane. Diir was calling the hyperactive little gnome "Elder," and was referring to himself as "Soveliss." Mialee considered Zalyn and her new, scholarly speech pattern. The little gnome returned her look with one of apology and tucked a lock of hair behind one pointed ear.

Mialee closed her eyes, put a palm to her temple and wished for the hundredth time that elves could sleep. She was getting a headache.

The elf called Clayn turned and pressed a few torn scraps of paper, already partially covered in elf-script, into her hand.

"Tornado honeybee, alacrity," Mialee thanked the ranger and took up the quill.

Her nimble fingers scrawled a few words on the paper. Mialee felt a wash of relief when she saw she could read them, and they made sense. Devis read the words aloud, reading over her shoulder. Apparently this pernicious magic Hound-Eye had given her didn't affect her fingers. She tried to remember how many spells she could cast without speaking, but there were only a few. A few was better than none.

" 'Where am I?' " the bard read. " 'How did I come back? Elder? Soveliss?' " As Mialee scribbled rapidly, the bard added, " 'Are those zombies outside?' "

Devis regarded Mialee with a third of his practiced, lopsided grin. "Oh, the easy stuff."

The elf woman gave him an irritated but gentle shove. She wasn't going to write the fact down for all to read, but Mialee found Devis's steady presence strangely comforting, even if the bard couldn't understand her when she talked and wouldn't take this seriously.

Zalyn turned to Clayn. "Clayn, how much time do I have?"

The ranger put an eye to a small gap in the boards over one window for a few seconds. He counted silently. When the elf turned back to Zalyn, he said darkly, "I estimate an hour, maybe two. They have already drawn closer. The turning cannot last much longer. I hope Ehlonna is prepared to grant us a reprieve one more time."

"I'll ask her," the gnome said, smiling, and Mialee realized the little cleric was giving orders. "Please keep an eye on them and alert me as soon as they breach the divine protections. The temple is lost, but Ehlonna's chosen make their own places of worship," Zalyn told the elf, who resumed his lookout at the boarded window.

The little gnome fingered the holy symbol around her neck absently. Mialee blinked. Zalyn no longer wore the crescent of Corellon Larethian. The over-sized medallion the cleric now wore bore a carving that depicted a rearing unicorn beneath branching boughs—the symbol of Ehlonna, goddess of the wood.

"It appears we have been given a gift of time," Zalyn said. "While we wait for your voice to recover, Mialee, perhaps it's time I revealed to you who I really am, what you're doing here, and why we risked returning you to life in this place. First, I should tell you that I have been the sole occupant of the temple of the Protector— actually an ancient temple of Ehlonna, our sacred Mother—for nearly a hundred years. There are no brothers or high clerics. I brought you back."

The gnome muttered an arcane spell, Mialee noted, then suddenly bent and aged before Mialee's eyes. She had become the withered, tiny crone from the Silver Goblet. Mialee could see now that the stinky little "prophet" was in fact an ancient, shriveled elf. The question was, which was the illusion—the gnome, or the crone?

Mialee's eye grew wide. "Saddlebag, albino," said the elf woman, forgetting to write. "Saddlebag."

Cavadrec's tattered, purple robes billowed behind the tall wight as he stalked down the corridor. The angry howls and horrible cries of a thousand different undead animals echoed deep underground. Hooked claws swiped at the fast-moving wight as he passed through the cages.

The wight hoped to save this part of his plan for the end, but recent events convinced Cavadrec that the time for this scheme to be unleashed was now. His pets would easily keep the only real threat to himself—that damned sword, Mor-Hakar, and the elf who wielded it—from reaching this lair before Cavadrec could drain the fool Favrid and complete his spell of dominion. While he found it extremely doubtful that the elf alone could actually kill Cavadrec, the wight meant to take no chances. If the elf could not be destroyed, he could at least be prevented from finding Cavadrec until it was too late, either to stop Cavadrec or save himself.

At that hour, Cavadrec would drink the blood of Favrid and complete the holy incantations revealed to him by Nerull a thousand years ago. The reborn corpses of every living thing that had ever died violently in the shadow of Morsilath —human or animal, dwarf, halfling, or elf—would rise and walk the earth. Every last one of them would be at Cavadrec's command. They would spread over the world like a plague.

When all was complete, Nerull would elevate Cavadrec to the level of a god. The Reaper had told him so in dark whispers that slid through the wight's brain like oiled silk.

The wight reached the end of the wide aisle between his caged pets and wrenched the lever that released the doors. His wightling animals, ready to infect the world above—and more importantly, bolster the forces in and around Silatham, where he ordered them to go first—exploded from confinement and rushed out the maze of lava tubes lacing the region. Cavadrec whirled and returned the way he had come, wading through the mass of chaotic animals.

"Then something whacked me on the back of the head, and I woke up here," the bard finished. Devis insisted on relating the tale of their encounter with the wight before Zalyn explained herself.

"That was me," Clayn said with neither pride nor apology. "You looked like a crawling zombie, and smelled like one, too."

"Yeah, well, you might have said something before you pulled out the club, Cane," Devis muttered, rubbing the back of his skull.

"Clayn."

"Whatever."

"He'd have chopped your head off if I hadn't stopped him, Devis," Darji said.

Mialee scribbled with her quill and held up the note. "The 'prophecy'? Explain yourself, Z."

The Zalyn hag laughed, and the sound was nothing like the hacking, disgusting little creature they'd met before.

"One and one and one is three,

"One for the teacher, one is for me.

"The Buried rings a bell for thee,

"The Buried rings a bell for thee.

"Elf on my left, lute gold and prudent,

"Elf on my right, black-haired student,

"Elf yet to come, guardian true.

"One elf is the teacher,

"The last one is his muse."

Mialee sighed and rolled her eyes.

" 'Lute gold and prudent?' " Hound-Eye chuckled. "Are you serious?"

The crone cracked a grin. "I'm no poet, Hound-Eye, and I had to throw it together in a few days."

A con man himself, Devis still didn't get the game in this prophetic doggerel. "I think I get who the 'guardian true' is, and the rest. One of them is you, the other is Favrid. But why us?"

"Patience, please, all will be clear," Zalyn interrupted, and then turned to the silent elf woman.

Mialee had given up on speaking for now. Devis leaned one hip on the wooden table and crossed his arms, standing protectively beside Mialee. The bard didn't like this Clayn at all, even if he had apparently protected this family of elves all by himself against a village full of zombies for a full day with nothing but two swords and a dwindling stock of arrows. Devis didn't trust the man. Or maybe he just didn't like the way Mialee looked at him.

When did I become possessive? Devis wondered.

It was a silly question to ask. The bard knew exactly when he had sworn to protect Mialee. Unfortunately, he hadn't succeeded the first time. He was glad to have a second chance.

That was life, Devis thought. And death. And life again. He wondered idly what Mialee had seen while her spirit was absent from her body.

"Favrid told me your opinion of prophecy, Mialee, and I tend to agree with you. The prophecy was for Devis's benefit. I knew that Soveliss was headed to Dogmar and was likely to be locked up by our fair and just and paranoid constable. I needed to let you know, Mialee, that you and the man you called 'Diir' would meet. I also hoped, Devis, that you might find the idea of a prophecy intriguing from a financial perspective."

"How did you know I'd get thrown . . . in . . . you little weasel! You ratted me out to Muhn."

"Griffon doorjamb?" Mialee was livid.

"I assure you I did not expect them to find you where they did," Zalyn confessed, embarrassed, "but Soveliss had to be free, and I knew you couldn't resist Gunnivan's old shatter spell."

"He's dead. How do you know Gu—"

"I'll never be able to explain all this if you don't stop asking me questions," the ancient elf woman said with a wink. Devis closed his mouth and decided it would be more pleasant to watch Mialee fume. She wore fuming well.

"A thousand years ago, the great alliance of clerics and wizards confined the prisoner, Cavadrec, beneath the mountain we now call Morsilath," Zalyn began.

She settled into a large, cushioned chair, one of the last pieces of unbroken furniture in the room.

Devis listened. Despite his extreme irritation over Zalyn getting him tossed in the clink on purpose, prophecies and great alliances made excellent material for epic ballads.

And the cleric had resurrected Mialee, so he found it hard to stay angry at the little woman. The crone grinned, but a sadness remained in her eyes.

"Devis, Gunnivan led us to you long ago, early in your career and before his death, and we have kept watch on you. If you accept this challenge, I promise you will sing a spell heard through all the planes."

"Really. Do these planes have any money, by any chance?" Devis replied. "You could have mentioned you knew Gunnivan, and that you're, you know, a thousand year old midget."

"I told you why I concealed my identity," Zalyn said with sudden authority. She smiled at the bard. "Trust me."

Bards that starred in their own epics could sack a lot of gold, and now he could honestly say that several dozen witnesses had heard that his 'coming was foretold.' He could make this work. To hear about a hero was cathartic or inspiring, to meet one could awe the average commoner and open the purse strings of genteel nobles seeking to impress their peers. The matrons of Dogmar alone might set Devis up for life. He shifted and nodded. He'd hear the little elf out.

"It is difficult to know where to begin," Zalyn said, looking less and less like a horrible crone and more like a simple, sad, tired old woman. Her eyes gazed distantly at a memory none of them could see. "As usual, the beginning is appropriate. Mialee, did Favrid teach you through lessons from his own past, as is the custom of Silatham wizards? Did you know he was from this village?'"

The elf woman nodded once, then shook her head.

"And the Buried One, Cavadrec?"

Mialee again shook her head no and blurted, "Beltbuckle pie?"

"Dear, dear," Zalyn muttered, "I told him so many times that you were ready. Then I don't imagine he told you how he shaped your studies to prepare you for this eventuality. You should have visited this place long ago. Favrid is one of the most intelligent men I've ever met," Zalyn said, "but he would forget his spell components if his familiar didn't remind him."

"She's right there," Darji chirped.

"Mialee, I need to tell you something about myself. You may have noted," said Zalyn, touching a finger to her pointed left ear, "my true nature. I am an elf. A very, very old elf. But I am not quite this old."

Zalyn whispered a spell in which Mialee picked out illusory components—arcane magic, not divine. So Zalyn had more than one field of study, in addition to being much more than a novice.

Zalyn finished her spell and raised her chin. Her features were still wrinkled with age, but they were noble and graceful, and her eyes glinted with youth. She produced a ribbon from her robes and tied her long strands back into a silver ponytail.

"Unfortunately," she said, "I never was very good at disguising my ears."

"You see," Zalyn continued, "I can speak so of Favrid because I've known him for a very, very long time. He's my *thirimin*."

" 'There-a-mint?' " Hound-Eye blurted.

"It means they're married," Devis clarified.

"Oh," Hound-Eye said, and squinted his good orb at Zalyn. "He halfling-sized, too?"

"Hardly," Zalyn said with a look that made Hound-Eye fidget.

Mialee felt Devis shift closer to her as he leaned against the table. Mialee had been staring at the point where the back of Devis's leather trousers made contact with the table, and shook her head.

"Favrid and I have been wed for a thousand years. We found thirimin together when we fought the Buried One. Before he was buried," said Zalyn, "as Favrid and I formulated the method that would allow us to defeat Cavadrec. The plan that the three of you and the two of us, Favrid and me, will attempt to make reality. To defeat the Buried One, instead of simply confining him, we must take a new tack."

Mialee looked at Devis, who frowned. What had he expected, that they'd be conjuring pancakes for the downtrodden of Dogmar?

"Wait," Devis said, "you said you had to hide your identity from us. What's your name?"

"Zalyn will do. I have used it for centuries. The Buried One would know me by a different name, one I won't bother to mention, lest Cavadrec hear you say it at a bad time," the little elf explained.

"Something like, 'I can't believe we're being killed and eaten by a wight that so-and-so roped us into fighting with a bit of improvisational prophecy?' Something like that?" Devis asked.

Zalyn smiled. "Something like that.

"The Buried One was once a colleague of Favrid's and mine," Zalyn went on, then turned pointedly to Devis, "and Gunnivan's."

Beside her, Mialee felt Devis start.

"The Buried One was once a cleric of the Mother, an elf named Cava. We learned, traveled, and fought together. Gunnivan rallied our spirits, Cava was the expert in spiritual dangers. Favrid and I explored arcane magic. Cava performed the bonding ceremony when Favrid and I decided to join. No others would marry a pair of 'eighty-year-old striplings.' Even then, Silatham had a tendency toward knee-jerk traditionalism." Zalyn smiled.

"The four of us were inseparable comrades. We traveled, fought, and learned together. But Cava deceived us all. We didn't know it, but he had been studying without us. He abandoned Ehlonna—" Zalyn jerked her thumb at a boarded window— "somewhere inside that mountain, which we called Kesirsilath back then. He found a source of tremendous, frightening knowledge. He secretly embraced the Hater of Life, whose name I shall not utter in our sanctuary.

"One day, while traveling through the far southern forest, we discovered an ancient tomb of a great high cleric of Moradin. Favrid and I, of course, wished to explore the find. No dwarves have lived in the far south for millennia, and the secrets it may have held . . ."

"Forget dwarves, I've never heard of any 'Great Southern Forest,' either," Hound-Eye growled. "There's nothing down there but sand."

"Believe me, I'm aware of the discrepancy, Hound-Eye." Zalyn said, "I was there when the desert was created."

Mialee couldn't quite make out what the halfling thief muttered in reply, but it sounded something like "smart-arsed immortal bastards."

"Cava refused to enter the tomb," Zalyn said as Hound-Eye stewed. "At first, he simply insisted we did not have time, then tried to convince us it was too dangerous. We thought he'd gone mad, or fallen under the sway of a fear spell. We had faced far more difficult challenges together in our adventures, and Cava was no coward. Gunnivan tried to break any fear effects with an inspiring ballad, in fact, but Cava simply grew more and more angry.

"Finally, Cava exploded. Before our eyes, the sapling staff in his hands twisted into a blackened thing, topped by a skull and scythe. The icon of the Reaper." Zalyn shuddered and looked every one of her thousand-odd years. "Cava told us to call him 'Cavadrec.' We barely escaped with our lives."

"I can see where this is going," Hound-Eye interjected. "You're telling me that the desert—that big one—some death worshipper did that trying to kill you?"

"Yes," Zalyn said, making no acknowledgement of the halfling's skeptical look and closing her eyes. "So much death. I can still hear the forest scream as the trees blackened and crumbled to dust. Cavadrec—" she spat the name— "he must have thought that if his new lord destroyed all life for a hundred miles, it would take care of the witnesses to his treachery. But he forgot about the god he'd so casually tossed aside."

Zalyn thumbed the golden icon around her neck. "As the wave washed over everything in its path, rolling after us, I took up the holy symbol of Ehlonna the fiend had cast away. I can't explain the certainty that filled my being to one who has never experienced it, but I felt Ehlonna of the Forest speak to me for the first time. She was horrified at the reckless destruction of so much of herself—the lifeblood of the forest. As soon as I touched this very medallion, Ehlonna sent an invocation through me. She shielded us from the Reaper, but could not save the rest of the forest. From that day forward, I devoted my life to three things—Ehlonna, my thirimin, and stopping Cavadrec."

"Did a great job on that, really," Hound-Eye snorted, but the others ignored him.

"Cavadrec went on a rampage. He called the dead into his service wherever he went. His armies slaughtered tens of thousands. Most ended up in his ranks." Zalyn closed her eyes again at the painful memory. "We did our best to fight him, but his secret studies made him far more powerful than any on our side. The noble Silatham Rangers died in droves. Farmlands became fetid swamp. The besieged common people—elves, dwarves, everyone—began to whisper that Ehlonna had given up and no longer watched over the Silath wood. In a way, they were right," she acknowledged uncomfortably, "for in the attack that nearly killed Favrid, Gunnivan, and me, Ehlonna was . . . wounded, if a god can be described that way. Savagely injured by the confrontation with the power of the Hater of Life. Ehlonna had not abandoned us, but had retreated to lick her wounds, sparing me what power she could for my efforts, but not enough to stop Cavadrec's onslaught.

"The last of us who stood against the dark were eventually forced back and bottled up in Silatham. Cavadrec and his armies of the dead surrounded us. Dogmardrukar, the northern dwarven settlement on the far side of Kesirsilath, already lay in ruins. From there, however, came hope."

"I don't think the word 'hope' is in the average Dogmari's vocabulary," said Devis.

"Not anymore, I agree, but a thousand years ago a high dwarven cleric of Moradin survived the slaughter and fought his way to besieged Silatham. With the combined power of Moradin and Ehlonna—mountain and forest, stone and soil—we sealed Cavadrec beneath Morsilath. We would have been lost if not for high cleric Muhn."

For the second time in as many minutes, Devis started beside Mialee. "Muhn? You're kidding."

"I assure you I am not," Zalyn said. "You can see how the destruction of Dogmardrukar and the descent of Dogmar into crime and corruption has affected the family line."

"Elder, I would not think to interrupt," Diir spoke for the first time in an eternity. "But—well—what about me? You told me that my name was 'Soveliss,' that I am from this place, which I can feel is true, and that this," he patted the short sword on his belt, "is needed to fight the Buried One."

"Yet I also said that we are old friends, did I not?" Zalyn said, eyes suddenly twinkling. Mialee recognized the look on Zalyn's altered face—as a "gnome," she'd worn the same expression when Devis suggested they raid the armory at the temple of the Protector.

"Soveliss, I say we are old friends, and I meant that literally. A millennium ago, you fought at our side."

"What?" Devis exclaimed. "Diir isn't a day over a hundred! Look at the guy."

"The sword you carry, Soveliss," Zalyn continued, "is called the Mor-Hakar. The Death-Killer. After we sealed Cavadrec beneath the mountain—renamed Morsilath, mountain of death —"

Dungeons & Dragons

"Always thought that was because of all the wights," Devis interrupted.

"The wights, Devis, are there because of the Buried One," Zalyn explained. "They were unfortunate explorers who delved into the mountain and discovered his prison."

With Devis mollified, Zalyn continued her tale. "Soon after we imprisoned the Buried One, Favrid, Gunnivan, Muhn, and I learned that our solution for containing his evil was far from perfect. Moradin was more than enough to keep the fallen cleric underground, but Ehlonna can be capricious. She had been injured greatly by Cavadrec's savagery and needed time to heal after she helped us confine the madman.

"I'm afraid the Mother of Elves fell asleep," said Zalyn. "Wanderers in the tunnels below the forest were able to break into the Buried One's prison, as I said before. Ehlonna, more worried about the growth of trees than the confinement of a hated enemy, was not able to prevent their access. These hapless souls were converted by Cavadrec into wights and began wandering back into the world. These wights have plagued Dogmar and these woods for centuries. We elves of Silatham have kept them in check."

The bard nodded. "That explains why so few get out."

"Correct," Zalyn agreed. "The three of us realized we needed to destroy Cavadrec once and for all. He was, after all, an elf, and could easily live as long and Favrid and I intended to. Because of Ehlonna's distraction, however, we needed to bide our time for her to recover.

"You, Soveliss—or 'Diir' if you prefer, that's actually a pretty good joke—volunteered to help. The village could spare only one ranger after our battles with Cavadrec. You stepped forward, the commander of the last remaining troop. You were given the Mor-Hakar to hold, and Favrid proceeded to turn you and the sword into stone."

122

Diir—no, Soveliss, Mialee reminded herself—was stunned. Mialee didn't blame him. It wasn't every day you learned you'd been a statue for a thousand years, although it wasn't like his transformation was news.

"I am . . . a thousand years old?" said Soveliss. For the elf, his raised eyebrows were equivalent to anyone else's screaming fit.

"Chronologically, you are aged one thousand and ninety-three years," Zalyn replied, "but the preservation offered by your millennium of transmutation ensured that the Mor-Hakar and the power infused within by Ehlonna would never want for the steady hand of a Silatham Ranger. We buried you on the battlefield of Morkeryth, beneath the ruins of our last outpost to fall before Cavadrec surrounded Silatham. That's the same place where we ultimately confined him. Many, many bodies have been laid low beneath that hallowed ground. You were simply another body beneath the earth, but you held a critical part of Cavadrec's ultimate destruction."

Mialee scribbled a question on a scrap and shoved the paper under Zalyn's nose.

"Yes, he did," the diminutive elf nodded.

"Did what?" Devis said.

"Mialee asked if Favrid released Soveliss from petrifaction. Clayn tells me Favrid left Silatham a week ago. He planned to retrieve you, Soveliss, and bring you to Dogmar to meet the others. I was still in the temple, of course, but Favrid contacted me with telepathy. I warned him not to be foolish, to at least take Clayn with him, but he refused. He has the stubbornness of a millenarian. Cavadrec struck just as the spell to return Soveliss to us was nearing completion."

Mialee drew a finger across her throat quizzically.

"Yes, the spell failed to complete. Much of his mind was left as stone."

"I remembered this place," Soveliss said distantly. "I remember something like it, before this, I mean. And something else. It's close and urgent, but . . ."

Zalyn produced a pinch of something Mialee didn't recognize and tossed it into the air with a wave of her hand. The little elf intoned a brief incantation, and Mialee saw the twinkling-light aura of a transmutative field fan out from Zalyn's fingertips. The sparkling field wrapped around Soveliss's head like a turban, then dissolved through his helm and into his skull. Soveliss was dumb-struck, his face flooded with recognition of everything at once.

"Sorry I didn't do that earlier," Zalyn said apologetically, sounding like her young gnomish self. "It's been a long time since I've cast that spell, I had to study it this morning. And you have to admit this is more dramatic. Gunnivan would have liked it."

Diir/Soveliss's brow raised even higher as his eyes bugged at Zalyn. "I have a family!" he whispered.

"Yes," Zalyn said, inclining her head to Clayn.

"Shocked, shocked, I am," Devis said, and rubbed the knot on the back of his head. "They're nothing—ow—alike."

"Ellyra," Soveliss hissed lividly after a few tortured seconds, "She's, she's not here. And the children. Where are they, elder?"

Mialee was stunned. The familiar, peculiar Silatham accent was there, but a new man inhabited the elf's skin. The ranger—for he could be nothing else, Mialee thought—made an angry move toward the elder cleric.

Zalyn closed her eyes and bowed her head, and Clayn moved to put himself between his apparent ancestor and the little elf.

"They do not walk with the wightlings," Clayn said, placing a hand on Soveliss's shoulder and looking him in the eye. "They all died over a hundred years ago, in the woods north of Silatham." The ranger grimaced. "Wolf attack. Nothing supernatural about it, maybe that's why we didn't expect it." Clayn's gaze narrowed at Zalyn, and it held a hint of the same fire that Soveliss barely held in check. "I was only ten."

"He was the only survivor," Zalyn said sadly. "But it was not a random attack. I fear it was something more. It is tied to the reason our enemy proves nearly indestructible."

"Excuse me, your eldership," Hound-Eye growled, "I've 'destroyed' an elf or two. It don't take a magic elf-sticker. You people bleed like anyone."

Every elf in the room—along with the one bird—frowned at the scruffy little man in bloody furs, even Devis, who had heard all about the halfling's elf-fighting exploits. Clayn actually let his swords clear a full inch of their scabbards.

"Well, I have. You ain't all just about life and goodness, are you? I killed elf bandits what tried to kill me and mine. Any of you'd done the same," Hound-Eye retorted. "And anyway, this feller isn't an elf anymore, is he? He's a bloody wight of some kind. I've killed wights, too." He opened his palms outward. "No magic."

"Hound-Eye, please accept my apologies. The rangers were forced to take action against those who would disturb the Buried One, and your people —"

"Apology, hell! You bloodless sons of kobolds killed any halfling you found more'n a mile outside Tent City," Hound-Eye barked.

Mialee thought he might actually draw his pick, but he simply clenched his fists.

Zalyn darkened and locked her gaze at the little man's good eye with a scowl wholly out of place. "You exaggerate, Hound-Eye. Your people—and many others, I'll grant you—were trying to burrow into the mountain for a cache of riches that never existed," she snapped, jamming her finger in the halfling's face. "We gave up trying to warn your people away hundreds of years ago, and resigned ourselves to killing any who were found before they could become Cavadrec's servants. The loss of every one of those lives wounded me as deeply as the Buried One wounded Ehlonna. I am sorry for your loss. Either do me the courtesy of sparing me your self-pity or restrain yourself. If you cannot do so out of respect for those you claim to have held so dear, you're welcome to take the matter up with the dead of my village."

Hound-Eye blinked and backed down.

Zalyn relented. "You are not to blame for the death of Tent City, halfling, but neither are we. Nor do I blame you for the deaths of any rangers, and I think the others accept that as well. We have all been pawns of circumstance." Hound-Eye reddened, and turned from the rest of them as he began to shake. Zalyn placed a hand on the little man's fur-covered shoulder, whispered a soft prayer, and magically calmed the halfling. As he turned to crouch on the floor, however, Mialee saw that his face was covered in wet tears, though his jaw was clenched. The halfling loudly blew his nose on his sleeve.

"Hound-Eye has a very good point, friends, and is wise," Zalyn continued. "No, most elves do not require magical power to pass into the beyond. Wights are vile horrors created from luckless innocents, but not close to the threat posed by the Buried One.

"Those who choose to follow the divine callings of the clergy usually focus our studies in two or three specific fields of specialty. This ideology varies from believer to believer, but is as common as it is pragmatic. I'm not saying I have laurels from the 'school of Good' or a 'doctorate of herbology.' I specialize, as does the Buried One.

"His first calling is obvious," said Zalyn.

"Death," said Devis.

"Needlepoint," said Mialee. She meant to say "Necromancy."

"Of course. But more perniciously, he uses and even inhabits animals," Zalyn said. "He's obsessed with taking all of Ehlonna's children away from her, and knows that for every creature he corrupts with the living death, the more difficulty Ehlonna has regaining her strength. He still is a blight on her soul."

"We noticed," Hound-Eye said. They'd all become intimately familiar with undead fauna.

"Surprised he hasn't made zombie trees," Devis cracked.

"Before he fell under Nerull's sway, animals and their ways were Cava's primary focus, not trees, mercifully. He mastered methods of moving his consciousness from animal body to elf body and back again. He can split himself into a group of individuals, act as a collective organism or a group of independents, yet retain a powerful, fully conscious presence within a primary body. He turned that power against us, and it made him all the more difficult to destroy. In fact, the body he wore when we confined him beneath Morsilath was the seventh elf-form he had stolen, that we knew of.

"He knew of the existence of the Mor-Hakar, learned of it from his foul spies, but did not reckon your peculiar situation, Soveliss. The attack on your family was part of Cavadrec's effort to capture the weapon before it could be used against him.

"Favrid and I managed to retrieve little Clayn's body before the wolves could, er, consume it," Zalyn gulped, "and I was able to bring him back from the beyond. Not quite as I did with you, Mialee. I have learned much in the intervening years. The boy was weak, but he survived, and has grown to into a strong ranger." Clayn looked at the floor.

"Favrid always believed in redundant protection," Zalyn added with a smirk, "and Cavadrec believed in the permanence and inevitable power of death. Favrid and I underestimated the Buried One, and we must hope he underestimates us as well."

Pell, the elf whose home this was, spoke for the first time. The man's voice was strident and inflected with something that told the elf woman he would welcome death himself if not for the presence of his family.

"Animals. That's what happened to us. The village was overrun with rats, a swarm of them. They came out all at once. Everyone they bit became a . . . I don't know what." Pell's soulless lack of emotion reminded Mialee of a clay golem. "I've seen wights, we all have. The rats, they didn't make people into wights. They're worse, they're rotten corpses. They eat anything, including each other. It's something slow. A wight kills you, you become a wight. This . . . you watch someone rot before your eyes. They just leave, and you're left with . . . you're left . . ." The robed man trailed off and he pulled his thirimin and remaining child close. It was apparent what happened to those bitten by the undead rodents, and equally apparent Pell had seen it happen to his own progeny.

Zalyn frowned. "His creations have certain powers of both wight and zombie—semi-intelligent 'wightlings,' if you will. It's what Favrid called them," Zalyn said. "Like wights, the Buried One's minions can convert a living being into creatures like themselves, but wights must completely kill the living thing to do so. Cavadrec concocted a necromantic technique that causes eventual conversion from a single bite. The victim need not die. However, the effect does take time. Minutes in the worst cases, hours in others."

"The rats went for the Rangers first, while they slept," Clayn said. "They took the barracks completely by surprise. My men and I, and maybe three or four other units, were in the field on patrol or we would have been caught, too. As it is, I am the last ranger in Silatham that I know of." He glanced at Soveliss. "Until now."

Devis turned back to Zalyn, puzzled. "You said you buried this guy, Cadavrink or whoever, in an elf body. But that was no elf we fought on the road. It was a wight. At least, it looked like a wight, but it was far more powerful than any other I've heard of."

"Yes, it is something we feared, but never believed Cavadrec would be mad enough to try. I know not how, but he inhabits a wight body. This is unexpected, and complicates matters even more. Favrid, I think, somehow held out a small belief that when the Buried One finally saw his destruction staring him in the face, our old friend Cava would return to us. But Cava, it appears, is completely gone, having joined the ranks of the undead. I believe he means never to breathe air again. That is why my thirimin is captive now."

Mialee scribbled and handed a note to Devis. "He expected to find either a living elf in a fresh body or an old elf in an old body," the bard read, and added on his own, "but he got jumped by a Cavadnik in a wight body."

Responding to some distant sound only he heard, Clayn turned and pressed his eyes to the slit in the boarded window.

"Elder, I think—"

That was all he managed to say before a fat, oily, hollow-eyed rat wriggled through the crack and scrambled atop the man's golden helm.

Then rats were streaming into the room from every conceivable crevice. Little Nialma, Pell's daughter, screamed. Smoking wightling rodents wriggled around the open flames in the fireplace, forcing Pell's terrified family to stumble to the center of the room. His wife Delia nearly collided with Clayn, who flung the helm off with his left hand and brandished a long sword in the other. Soveliss had both swords out even faster, and he skewered the rat and Clayn's helmet with the Mor-Hakar. Devis scrambled to his feet, knocking his lute to the floor with an atonal clamor of strings as he struggled to free his sword. Hound-Eye nailed a rat to the floor with his pick. Mialee plucked the wand from her belt in a heartbeat. She dared not risk speaking a spell, but she could mentally invoke the missiles in the wand. With her right hand, she drew her rapier and batted at another chittering rodent. Zalyn, as near as Mialee could tell, was doing absolutely nothing but standing like a statue.

Slow, insistent thuds resounded through the little room's weird acoustics. Mialee thought it sounded like a dozen drunks trying to open a tavern after closing time. Several of the boards nailed haphazardly over the round windows snapped, and gray, ragged, half-rotten arms clawed the air inside their sanctuary.

Mialee gritted her teeth, kicking a hollow-eyed rat off her boot with a snarl. The last living people in Silatham tensed for the inevitable intrusion of the walking dead. She held the wand overhead and sent a small missile blast into an unseen body at the end of one of the grasping hands. A scream and flash of flame outside the window testified that she hit her mark.

Zalyn finally moved. The little elf, her back to Mialee, raised the golden symbol of Ehlonna overhead. "*Ehlonna hinue, mormhaor shan!*" the tiny cleric bellowed in a booming, supernatural voice.

Metallic, gold-flecked, green energy shot in every direction from the holy icon. Mialee felt gentle coolness spread through her body in the hot, confined space.

Every rat in the room burst with a splatter of orange fire and hot gore. They flamed into cinders within seconds, leaving smoldering guts all over the room. An unholy chorus of hideous, rasping shrieks erupted around the tiny little house, and the mangled talons flailing into the room jerked back as one. Many of them, Mialee noted with disgust, left dripping strips of flesh hanging from jagged boards. Even a few clawed hands dropped to the floor and twitched momentarily before flaming out like the rats.

Zalyn turned and faced the wizard. She looked suddenly drawn and frail, and her breathing was heavy and erratic. Still, her eyes twinkled as she spoke.

"I've given you all a lot to take in. There is more, but the night has already gone on far too long. Ehlonna will give us her protection for a few more days. We all need rest. Tomorrow, we can discuss plans."

Mialee retrieved her charcoal and paper, which had fallen to the floor. She scribbled.

"Favrid?" Zalyn asked, and looked like her heart would break. "He knows the Buried One dare not kill him for a few more days. As I said, he has grown very stubborn in his old age. As long as Darji remains, I will know he lives. And as long as Favrid lives, there is hope. Think on that, child. One thing, though."

Mialee nodded.

Zalyn pointed to Mialee's pack, resting under the table. "I'd recommend you meditate, then take time to study and prepare yourself. We will rest, and soon, you will recover you words. You must."

A sober hush fell over their little band of survivors. The only sounds that reached Mialee's ears were of the crackling fire, the bawling of the terrified little girl, the distantly screaming zombies, and the reverberating thuds of Clayn and Soveliss pounding the barricade back into place with the butts of their swords.

Mialee sneezed twice into her spellbook and went into another coughing fit. Devis sat on the floor beside her, noodling around with a new ballad on his lute, and sympathized. Between the festering rat residues already buzzing with tiny flies, the days-old gore encrusting everyone's clothes, and the foul, but necessary, waste bucket in the corner, drawing breath in their little sanctuary was a dangerous adventure. Devis set aside the lute and opened his leather vest. Most of his under-tunic was still clean, at least relatively so. He shrugged and tore two wide strips from the bottom, tied one around his own nose and mouth—winced at how long it had been since he'd taken a bath—and offered the other to Mialee. She looked at the rag with distaste, but relented after she sneezed violently one more time.

"Thistle—" Mialee frowned, and said more slowly, "Thanks, garlic."

She sighed with a weak grin and tied the covering over her lower face. She shifted closer to him and placed a hand on his knee as she returned to her spellbook. Devis looked over her shoulder—he couldn't make out the details, but it looked like she was studying ways to make things disappear.

"It's always easier to surprise someone when they can't see you," Devis said.

Mialee looked up at him in mild irritation, and scooted a few inches away, turning the book's spine to the bard.

"All right, all right," Devis said, and resumed work on his new melody, plucking idly.

It had been nearly a day since Zalyn annihilated the swarming rats and sent the wightlings packing, for a while. Hound-Eye and Nialma played in one corner—the halfling would bark the name of an animal, and the little girl would pretend to be the animal. She was giggling, and Devis was gratified to see his old pal Hound-Eye had actually begun coming back from the dark place he'd inhabited since Takata's death at the bridge. The little girl particularly loved to play pretend rat, which seemed to disturb her mother and father, but the girl was giggling and laughing. Pell had opened up a bit, and Devis learned that the man was a scholar. He and his family had just returned to Silatham when the wightling rats struck the sleeping town. Now Pell's family was less than half the size it had been a week ago.

Humming over the idle notes, Devis's thoughts turned to something more pleasant. He regarded the elf woman beside him out of the corner of his eye.

Mialee confused the daylights out of him. Obviously, Devis had grown attached to her during the journey south, and thought that she just might have been feeling the same way. His instincts about such things were usually sharp. Then, the wight attacked and unexpectedly killed her and shattered him.

After Mialee's return to life, she and the bard joked with each other, shared a few awkward moments, but Devis sensed her mind was distant. It wasn't just the residual effect of Zalyn's aphasia potion. Occasionally, as when she touched his knee and called him "garlic," he closed the distance, but she drew back as soon after.

As his fingers played over the strings, Devis speed-picked a progression of chords he had never played before, a collaboration of notes that created a sound entirely new, yet as familiar as a timeless hymn. The bard smiled beneath his ersatz facemask. The hook was exactly what the ballad needed. It just took time for such things to emerge from the jumble of random melodies in his fingers.

As the song's magic surrounded him with simple, twinkling lights that flitted about the room like fireflies, the wightlings seemed very far away, even as the corrupted, rotten victims of Silatham screamed and howled outside in the early morning. The air itself seemed to get cleaner, if only a little, an unanticipated side effect of the new spell song.

Zalyn's face was drawn and sallow, and her breath came in steady, pained wheezes. She leaned against Clayn, who had leaped to her side when she began wobbling. Devis saw that she clutched the golden symbol of Ehllona in tiny, white-knuckled hands. Acrid, foul-smelling rat-smoke drifted through the hot, cramped room.

The elder of Silatham had just turned back another wightling onslaught. There had been fewer rats but more humanoids, and something new, at least inside Silatham—vultures and wolves, dozens of them.

The barricade was badly damaged. Devis, Pell, Soveliss, and Mialee raced to pound the cracked and broken boards back into place.

"It seems," Zalyn said as Clayn helped her to a seat on the floor, "my usefulness is beginning to wane."

"Elder," Clayn began, "Holy Ehlonna will protect us. She must find a way to—"

"Ehlonna is not the problem, dear, brave Clayn," Zalyn said wearily as the ranger crouched beside her. Devis wished he could help the old woman with an uplifting poem, but dared not stop his efforts on the windows.

"Moradin," Clayn spat, "he betrayed us. Released the Buried One before the Mother was ready."

"No, if anything, Moradin has done more than his fair share. Do not speak ill of the Dwarffather, only his strength kept the Buried One in check while Ehlonna convalesced," Zalyn smirked.

"The problem is not with the gods, my boy," she said with resignation. "It's with me. I am dying."

Everyone in the room froze. Devis winced as a heavy, jagged chunk of table dropped painfully on his toe, but he bit back a yelp.

"Don't all of you look at me like that. I am well over eleven hundred years old. Even among elves, I am ancient. The effort of fighting back so many of the Buried One's minions has forced me to draw on my own strength as much as the Mother's," Zalyn smiled weakly, though Devis saw pain in her eyes. "Ehlonna does not share her gifts with the world lightly, and she always asks for them back. Favrid and I have led very long lives with the Mother's help. We had to, for the sake of our cause. But," she coughed, a wheezing hack that filled the bard's gut with sickening certainty, "we always planned to enter Ehlonna's embrace together. I fear he may have to catch up with me."

"You cannot die, Elder," Clayn insisted. "We will find a way to bring you back. You are all that stands—"

"Of course she's not," Soveliss interjected. "Anyone can die, Clayn. And not everyone gets a second chance," the ranger said, eyeing his grandson and Mialee darkly.

That surprised Devis, but he understood, he thought. His friend had lost his love and his children, and Zalyn had not been able to bring them back to life. Of course he resented the ones who returned. The bard sympathized, but hoped Soveliss would be able to overcome his bitterness soon. Devis missed Diir.

"He speaks the truth, ranger, and you know it," Hound-Eye said, looking away from little Nialma.

Zalyn said, "A soul must want to return from the beyond. Even a god cannot force a free spirit back to this world if it does not want to make the journey. My conscious mind keeps me fighting Ehlonna's call while I reside in this body, but once free of it, I fear that what I find beyond will be too much for this old soul to give up."

"Don't die, Elder," Nialma said.

"Little one, it is not something I can change. I wish there was some way you did not have to learn this, not at this age, but all things end." Zalyn grinned, and a gnomish twinkle appeared in her eyes. "But I will not leave you until you are safe. And when I am gone, Ehlonna will look after you, Nialma. I promise."

Devis pounded one last board into place and sniffed. For Nialma's sake as well as his own and everyone else's he hoped Zalyn's faith in Ehlonna was even half justified. The alternative was certain doom.

He heard a squawk from Darji and jumped. The little bird was back from her scouting mission, wriggling through one of the few openings left unblocked for ventilation. The raven still glowed with the soft, blue energy Zalyn had cast to keep Darji safe.

"I have word from Favrid, Elder," the little bird cawed. The raven chirped into Zalyn's ear while the elder nodded. The elf straightened, and some of her old strength seemed to return to her bent frame.

"Favrid is alive," Zalyn announced, "but restrained. I must think on this while I rest. This evening, we will speak further."

Zalyn promptly sat cross-legged, closed her eyes, and slipped into a state of meditation.

"Anyone have any dice?" Devis asked.

The day had been interminable. As the sunlight faded, making their little space even darker, Zalyn suddenly snapped out of her trance. Devis and Hound-Eye abandoned their efforts at teaching Nialma how to gamble, and they all gathered expectantly around the diminutive elf.

"Children, I apologize for leaving you," Zalyn said. "We have much to prepare for. The day of prophecy is close at hand."

"Says . . . you . . . banana," Mialee managed without looking up from her spellbook. She almost had the invisibility spell, she hoped. She wouldn't know until she tried, but it was the most useful spell she could think of that she could master in a short time.

"I admit," Zalyn croaked around another hacking cough, "I deceived you. But holy Ehlonna told me that she needed a millennium to recover, and I will not doubt her, capricious as she may be. We must act one thousand years to the day from that hour we sealed the Buried One beneath Morsilath. But Darji has just told me something chilling, something I needed time to cogitate on before I told the rest of you."

She composed herself, and Mialee and the others quietly shuffled around her to listen. For a split second, Mialee was reminded of the shambling movements of the walking dead. Even with a day of rest, the besieged group was showing signs of serious fatigue.

"What?" Hound-Eye blurted, shifting impatiently next to Nialma and her family.

"Just as we did not know of Cavadrec's transformation from elf to wight, we did not know that this day chosen by Ehlonna would allow Cavadrec to compound his betrayal."

"In Common?" Devis asked.

"Cavadrec has discovered a spell so terrible I am loath to describe it, but I must," Zalyn said sadly. "He has discovered a way to raise the bodies of all the fallen warriors buried at Morkeryth and turn them into a well-armed wightling army under his complete control."

"Why does he need a spell?" The bard pressed. "You said he used to do that all the time in the bad old days. He didn't need a special spell to do what he did to Silatham. You said he just sent in a bunch of rats."

"Never did he raise so many all at once, or such a pernicious group of corpses. Infectious wightlings are perfectly adequate to convert a living soul into the walking dead, but when I say the dead of Morkeryth, I speak of legends. The greatest of our elf heroes from the days before," Zalyn intoned. "Many of the most recent fell fighting his evil at our sides. Thousands upon thousands of Silatham rangers, dwarven battle clerics, human paladins lending the strength of their many gods, and the noble fighters of the Halfling Defense Corps." She eyed Hound-Eye knowingly, who nodded with a mix of horror and something like awe.

"There ain't no 'Halfling Defense Corps,'" Hound-Eye said. "My kind look after themselves, but we don't go in for armies."

"Not anymore," Zalyn said. "The Corps' ranks were decimated a thousand years ago. This region was forever changed by

Cavadrec's ravages, from the southern desert to the foul stench of Dogmar to your Tent City, my friend."

"What does . . . exact dandeli—date . . . have to do with anytrout?" Mialee said with effort.

"The thousand-year mark is the crux of the spell, as it is the length of time Ehlonna demanded. Cavadrec must carry out the incantations and mix the appropriate potions and poultices. That, I fear, is why he has taken Favrid and, Favrid tells me through his familiar, the reason my thirimin yet lives. Cavadrec lacks only one element to complete the spell and raise his army of darkness. The Buried One must drink the freshly-drawn blood of one living being who witnessed the fall of all those he wishes to raise."

Mialee gasped. "Feather," she whispered.

"Cavadrec was not aware, I believe, that he had two choices," she said, touching her fingertips to her breast. "My blood, too, would have worked. But he did not know I still lived. I have been hidden in the temple of the Protector for a long time, and we allowed the Buried One to believe I had died of old age." She smirked ironically, now she really was dying of old age.

"I suspect that playful Ehlonna has seen fit to make my contrived prophecy truth. I hope so, for if we fail, she will suffer the most of all," Zalyn replied. "Life will be replaced with living death. The world will fall under his sway, and the Hater of Life will reign supreme." She sounded more than a little like the crone prophet.

"Oh, just that," Devis cracked, but no one laughed. He grimaced, then asked, "So what must we do, Zalyn?"

"Clayn," Zalyn nodded at the ranger and pointed at a dusty, forgotten chest bigger than Hound-Eye, tucked far beneath the battered and broken wooden table.

"Certainly, Elder," Clayn said, and dragged the chest so that it sat before Zalyn. She whispered a short prayer and sprinkled a bit of some green powder on the trunk's heavy lock, which disappeared in a magical flash. The lid popped open of its own accord, and the others stood and gathered behind the cleric.

Mialee's jaw dropped. She didn't' recognize everything in the trunk—planes, was that a lute?—but it looked like a small treasure trove of scrolls, weapons, and artifacts.

"Not all components of our 'prophecy' were turned to stone and buried on the battlefield," Zalyn said with a gnomish giggle. "Some have been here, in my home, for safekeeping."

Mialee blinked. She hadn't realized they'd been hiding in the house her teacher had shared with his thirimin. Looking around now, though, she saw that the place bore definite signs of Favrid's absentminded decorative style, if one could call it that.

"First," Zalyn said proudly, "is this lute." The little elf pulled the instrument from the jumble of objects. She turned and extended the elegantly engraved instrument, which looked worn with age, to Devis. "I hope you won't mind, Devis," she said with a grin.

Devis looked as if he'd seen a ghost. He goggled at the lute, but slowly held out his hands to take it. He slung the strap over one shoulder and picked a melancholy chord that rang throughout the room.

"Gunnivan," he whispered, gazing at the carvings in the golden wood.

"Yes, it was his," she said. "With this lute, Gunnivan's music helped us inspire Ehlonna herself to overcome her injuries and seal the Buried One in his prison. Tomorrow, you will use it to help me coax her into action with . . ." She rustled around amongst the objects, "this."

She held out an ancient scroll, which the bard accepted and unrolled. He gaped once more. Mialee guessed this was the bard's day for surprises.

"Gunnivan wrote this!" Devis gasped. The old bard had been dead for so many years, Devis thought he'd learned all of his mentor's secrets years ago.

"Indeed," Zalyn said, "with my help, and Favrid's. But I think you'll recognize the soul of the piece is his."

Devis plucked the lute, lost in the quality of sound produced by the masterfully crafted instrument. Zalyn returned to her trunk and produced two more scrolls.

"This," she said, shaking the tube in her left hand, "is the sacred invocation I must use soon after Devis plays Gunnivan's music. With Ehlonna's full strength at our backs, this spell will break through the Buried One's unholy protections. This, on the other hand," she said, shaking her right fist, "will nullify Cavadrec's arcane devices and methods."

"He's a wizard, too?" Devis asked.

"He had a thousand years to study, as I have. But he also relies on many arcane artifacts."

"Like a helm that lets him disappear?" Soveliss asked.

"Exactly, ranger," Zalyn said. "Unfortunately, I ceased most of my arcane studies long ago, even if I weren't required to read the invocation of Ehlonna. I can read the scroll, any wizard could, but to ensure success, it must be Favrid. This is where you come in, Mialee. Favrid is restrained from using his hands, and you know that he never bothered studying how to summon magic without them. You must free him from the restraints however you can, and get this scroll into his hands. Darji tells me that they are mundane shackles. I imagine Cavadrec gets special pleasure out of holding Favrid just out of reach of his powers.

"I think the rest is clear," Zalyn finished, though she did not close the trunk. "Once the invocations are made, Cavadrec is still a wight, albeit trapped in the body for the first time in a thousand years. That is our chance to strike. At the moment Favrid finishes the nullification spell, you, Soveliss, must put the Mor-Hakar in the bastard's stinking brain."

"**That's all well** an' good for the 'chosen ones'," Hound-Eye blurted. "What about the rest of us?"

Zalyn smiled apologetically. "I fear your presence is as unintended as it is unfortunate," she replied.

"Well, if someone's going to put steel in the son-of-a-dog's eye, I'm in." Hound-Eye stood eye patch-to-eye with the little elf and clenched his fists. "And you ain't stoppin' me."

Devis grinned. He had hoped Hound-Eye would come along.

"And the rest of 'em?" Hound-Eye cocked his eye at Clayn and the family Pell. "What about little rat-girl?"

"I will stay to cover your backs," Clayn said immediately, "and protect the others."

"Who's going to cover *your* back, elf? The bird?" Hound-Eye asked. Devis could see he was beginning to panic at the thought of leaving Nialma in the hands of her catatonic parents and a single Silatham ranger.

"I will not be able to turn when we leave, Clayn. I must be at full strength to defeat the Buried One. You will be trapped in here. But Ehlonna will provide," Zalyn said.

"I've lasted this long," Clayn said. The bard could not have been more surprised at the next voice he heard.

"Halfling," Delia said in a monotone whisper, "take her. Take her, please. Get her out of here."

Hound-Eye went into a coughing fit, but managed to pound his chest and ask, "Gyah?"

"We have decided what we must do," Pell cut in suddenly. He turned to Clayn and stammered, "We will help you fight them, ranger. But you," he pointed at Hound-Eye, "will see to it that my daughter escapes, if you do."

Hound-Eye simply nodded, his one eye wide as Nialma slipped a tiny hand into his calloused palm. "Houndie!" the elf girl said, and started to make little barking noises.

Hound-Eye crouched—but not much—to take the girl by the shoulders. "You listen to me, rat-girl," he growled, "this is going to be bad. Maybe more bad than staying here. If you want to stay with your mama . . ."

"Houndie!" the girl said and wrapped the halfling in a gleeful hug.

"It's 'Hound-Eye,' kid," the halfling whispered.

"All right, then," Zalyn suddenly said. "We all know what we must do. Mialee, you will prepare spells focused on offense, freeing Favrid, and anything else that might be useful. Ah!" she exclaimed, remembering something, and ran back to her still-open trunk. She rummaged through the treasures within and produced a pitch-black wand with a red tip. Mialee's was almost out of charges after the last few days, Devis was willing to bet.

"Hey, Zalyn," Devis asked. Delia's desperate request had reminded him of something he could not believe he hadn't thought of before. "Are you going to teleport us into Morsilath?"

"Thought you'd never ask," Zalyn said, looking very much like her gnome-self. "Look at this." She crossed the room to the center of the floor, slapped three times with the butt of her hand, and stood back.

The center of the floor glowed orange for a moment, then disappeared. Hound-Eye had to hold Nialma back from jumping in.

"This leads to an ancient mining track. The tunnel will lead us right there. It is useless as an escape route," she said apologetically to Pell and Delia, "for it leads only to Cavadrec's prison and the hollow volcanic tubes that run out from beneath Morsilath. You are safer here with Clayn.

"We must not leave the cart track, for the lava tube network is a labyrinth. One wrong turn, and we would be lost forever."

"Elder!" Clayn suddenly hissed, pointing at the little cleric, wide-eyed. Everyone turned and stared at Zalyn, who froze. A small, gray rat with empty eyes finished wriggling from the shoulder of her robe. Before even the rangers had time to act, the wightling rodent sunk a pair of tiny incisors into Zalyn's exposed neck.

Zalyn screamed.

Soveliss was to her before Mialee could move and flung the foul thing off of the cleric's shoulder. It landed in front of Clayn, who stomped it flat.

Zalyn's eyes grew wide and Mialee saw her face become a faint shade of gray.

"How?" the little cleric whispered, and dropped to the floor.

A hideously familiar chorus of arrhythmic thumps pounded all around them as Mialee ran to the fallen Zalyn. The wightling elves had climbed back up the tree and now sounded like they covered Zalyn's tiny home like a swarm of nesting hornets.

"Devis!" she shouted, gratified that the bard whirled to join her. She might have said "dodo" a few hours ago.

Clayn, Soveliss, Pell, and Delia—Delia, Mialee blinked with amazement—dashed to the doors and windows. She didn't spot

Hound-Eye, but heard him whispering soft reassurances to little Nialma.

She rolled Zalyn over onto her back before she considered how foolish that might be—if Zalyn was already a wightling.

The little elf was drawn and injured, but as her eyes fluttered open, Mialee saw with relief that the elder's sockets still held the twinkling brown eyes she'd learned to trust.

"Mialee," she whispered weakly, "I am lost."

"No, you've got to fight," Devis said as the din outside grew into an incessant chorus of pounding, rotten fists and growling, mindless moans.

Mialee felt her eyes begin to well up. Though Devis was typically optimistic, she saw in Zalyn's face that the little woman spoke the truth.

"I will, Devis," Zalyn croaked, smiling bitterly at the bard. "Even now, I feel Ehlonna . . . lending me her strength against the plague. It was—"

The hacking cough shook her form, and Mialee helped her wipe away the black phlegm that dribbled down the side of her mouth.

"It was a small rat, a little bite," Devis said, growing more frantic. "You can handle that. You're the big-time elder, right? Right?"

"Right," Zalyn managed, but she looked far away.

A strange light flashed into her eyes, and suddenly she leaped to her feet, jaw clenched, but glowing with a faint, green halo of light. When she spoke next, her voice was strange. It sounded like Zalyn's voice, but layered beneath another, impossibly beautiful tone that immediately made Mialee feel a comforting warmth.

"Children, we must go. Ehlonna is ready. We are so close. We will hold off the Reaper that long."

Mialee and Devis gaped. "Is that—?" the bard stuttered.

"It is me, Devis," Zalyn smiled beatifically at the bard, and Mialee saw him smile in genuine awe as she felt her own jaw refuse to close. "And we are also a part of Ehlonna. This vessel is tainted, but must persevere. We will see the destroyer cleansed of our body by the morrow." Mialee wondered which one of the elf's occupants, the deity or the cleric, had said the last part. She opened her mouth to ask but before she had a chance, the little elf/god said, "Come. We go." She crooked a finger at them, then leaped into the nothingness in the center of the floor.

Chunks of wood flew into the room as the wightlings finally breached the long-abused defenses. Nialma's screams of terror were muffled by Hound-Eye's fur cloak.

"Get out of here!" Clayn shouted, slashing at the wightlings that crashed into the room.

Devis and Mialee scrambled to their feet as Soveliss and Darji followed the Zalyn/Ehlonna hybrid's example.

"Hound-Eye!" Devis shouted. The halfling was clutching Nialma, who was screaming at her parents.

Pell and Delia turned as one. Delia gave a small, sad wave to Nialma.

"Damn you halfling! Save my daughter!" Pell shouted as he took up a chunk of wood, turned, and cracked it against a grasping, clawed wightling arm.

"Come on, baby," Hound-Eye said as soothingly as he could to the confused little girl, and dropped into the hole clutching Nialma to his chest. His one eye widened at them, then he disappeared with a long, descending epithet that trailed off into the darkness below.

Mialee didn't have time to think about what they were jumping into because Devis put his arms around her shoulders and shoved her forward. She stepped out over the black pit and dropped like a stone.

Many wightling elves had clawed their way fully into the little room. Clayn, Pell, and Delia fought them back with the ferocity of a mother bear defending her young. Devis spared the desperate defenders one last look, clutched Gunnivan's lute to make sure it was strapped in place, closed his eyes, and jumped.

He fell for maybe five seconds before opening his eyes. Above him, he heard bold shouts of challenge and the screeching howls of the living dead. He was descending at a fairly relaxed speed down the inside of a long tube of woven athel wood. Orange light glowed from below and cast long, bizarre shadows all around him.

This escape hatch was magical. He looked down and could barely make out Mialee, falling at a slightly faster rate, but not apparently in danger. Beyond her, he could see tiny specks that must have been the others coming to a landing.

"Amazing, isn't it?" a voice chirped in his shoulder, and Devis inadvertently yelped. Darji flapped her wings slowly, turning cartwheels. "I feel like a hummingbird!"

Devis looked down and felt his stomach roll uncomfortably. The distance hadn't seemed real to him as he slowly descended, but seeing the bird zip around the tube made him reassess the distance.

"Gods," he whispered.

He still had to be at least a mile up. He hoped the orange glow he was seeing wasn't from an open magma flow.

Devis guessed it was a full two minutes before he finally felt stone beneath his feet. He stood at the head of a long tunnel that descended into blackness, lit by torches. Twin iron tracks ran the length of the narrow tube. A large mine cart stood before him. It was twice his height, and as big as a good-sized fishing boat, but without the charm. About a dozen barrels labeled with the Dwarvish words for "blasting powder" were stacked behind him, where the tunnel ended.

Screams, bellows, and howls echoed down the shaft above him, but he did not look. Devis could not have pulled his attention away from the rest of the area all around the hollowed-out unloading dock. The barrels of black powder, if they actually still held any, along with a surprising number of food crates and iron water tanks, were the only undisturbed containers in the cavern. Everything else had been methodically, almost insanely, destroyed.

The place was an absolute treasure trove of armor, weapons, and, well, treasure.

There were swords with more gemstones encrusted on the hilt than Devis had ever imagined could fit. Hammers, axes, pikes, picks, and elegant, unstrung bows lay everywhere. Gold and silver shields emblazoned with fascinating symbols Devis had only seen before in history libraries, others bearing the unicorn and tree of Ehlonna, were tossed in careless piles. A few empty suits of heavy dwarven plate, the hammer and anvil of Moradin embossed on their chests in platinum, sat in ghostly repose against a wall covered in silver, gold, and platinum. Sweet platinum. Coins of every denomination he had ever coveted and many more he'd never seen littered the ground. Crates and chests had been shattered and all the possessions inside strewn about and picked over.

Amongst the piles of gold, unsettling footprints marked where someone—or thing—on two legs had stomped through the lode. Devis had a disturbing feeling those tracks had not been made by any Silatham elves on a stroll through their siege hoarde. Despite their lousy luck at confining evil overlords, he had to give the elves credit. Everyone else in the world could turn into a wightling, and they just might be able to hold out. They might have, if the wightling plague hadn't started within their walls.

Devis must have been licking his lips, for only that could explain how badly he bit his tongue when a screech jumped out of the huge cart. He winced and pressed his lacerated tongue to the roof of his mouth. Nialma's little head poked over the edge of the cart above him. She was smiling with the resilience of youth and the joy of finding an enormous, new toy. She giggled and then disappeared.

Devis looked at the assorted riches and sighed, wincing at the cold air on his injured tongue. The money wasn't going anywhere, and he supposed if he didn't get moving he wouldn't ever be able to spend it anyway. Still . . . he crouched and scooped up a few handfuls of platinum coins and gemstones and slipped them into one of the bigger pouches on his belt.

As he rose, something metal smacked him on the forehead. A familiar silk rope and a supposedly collapsible grappling hook, still folded, hung in the air before him, dangling down from the lip of the cart.

The bard grasped the line and clambered up the smooth iron to join his friends, careful not to let the lute hanging at his hip scratch against the wall of the giant cargo mover and trying to remember where he'd left that rope.

Hound-Eye was in mid-sentence as Devis dropped with a clang and a boom to the bottom of the iron cart. "—don't you just zap us down there? Why the he—" The halfling eyed the giggling Nialma and continued, "Why are we in a giant cart, for—er—pity's sake? You're a goddess, ain't ya?"

"We are here to preserve this vessel," Zalyn said with a voice that betrayed very little of her real self. "The magic of the song is still required to grant us focus and allow me to suffuse dead Silatham." She turned to Devis without explaining the last. "It is time. We remember our obligation. This vessel did not know that we always watch over her. We do not need to be 'coaxed.' But we do love music, and we require inspiration." Devis felt himself melt before the goddess-Zalyn, and fumbled for the scroll pouch that held Gunnivan's ballad.

"Thankth, Zthalynth."

Devis blinked and worked his jaw, sticking out his bleeding tongue. "Oh tho! Youth'e goth tho be kithing thee. How ab I thuppothed thoo thig the thog? Thith ith thust thuthig geat!"

"What did he say?" Nialma asked.

"Nothig. Nothig," Devis snapped. "Oh, Tharlaghn abthidthes!

Then the frantic bard snapped up straight. "Wai, pothionth! Tthalynth, you hab the watht pothionth."

Zalyn—or Ehlonna?—stepped to Devis in a flash and waved a hand in front of his chin. Devis looked down at the pint-sized elf.

"*Hinual faenya,*" boomed a voice that filled the tunnel.

He felt warmth on his tongue and popped his mouth open. The injury was gone. At the same time, a desire to sing flooded through him, more powerful than any emotion he'd ever felt. Music surged up from his heart as Devis sang, and it flowed through his fingers into the lute as he played. He didn't know the words or the melody, yet as each note formed—no, as *he* formed each note and sang each word—it was perfect.

Zalyn took up the song, but she wasn't Zalyn. The shrunken, poisoned body of the elf was filled with Ehlonna and her voice was strong, youthful, and beautiful. Together their voices overflowed the rail cart that somehow seemed pitiably small now, they flooded the tunnel and rushed up the levitation shaft to the tiny, beleaguered house where Devis's friends fought for their lives against undead monsters.

He was awash in the sensation of wanting only to protect ten precious souls. He was connected to every one of them, feeling their terror, anger, resolve, and hope. Most of all he felt Zalyn, dying Zalyn, struggling to sustain her life against a black cloud of poison spreading through her exhausted, weakened body.

And there was one more . . . a distant, unfamiliar, but smiling heart Devis knew could only belong to Favrid.

Then through the song Devis felt the stirring of a new presence. It was far above them. Not human or elf, but animal and plant. Silatham was returning to life. The athel wood still felt the horror of the walking dead. But now the city itself would fight back and aid the trio high above Devis's head. Their courage blended with the courage of the goddess, who was so much more than just a spirit inside Zalyn. She suffused Silatham itself.

The wightlings that blighted Silatham sizzled and burned wherever they touched the enchanted wood. Any outside the enclosing walls simply dropped to the ground, lifeless at last. Those inside were trapped by Ehlonna and burned by her indignation.

But then Devis's concentration on the flowing music was snapped by a defening bellow from Clayn, far above him. Bodies and pieces of bodies of rats and zombies and wightlings plunged down through the chute above them.

A few twitching zombie parts and numerous rats landed in the cart, but Soveliss chopped and Hound-Eye smashed them into harmless chunks. Devis promptly slipped on the slickened floor and fell hard onto his back with a crunch. Desperately he pushed his back up the side of the cart and reached for the lute. He found it in two pieces, still connected by the strings. The bard couldn't know it, but he held the instrument exactly as he had held Mialee's body.

He stared at it, for the first time in his life so shocked he was unable to speak.

Zalyn spoke. "Devis, you did not need the song of Gunnivan. Your own muse gifted you with a voice that can charm a god all on its own." The elf-goddess's glowing features bunched into a gnomish grin, and she laughed. "It was not the lute! You did it! The power of Silatham is refocused. The athal trees are restored and Ehlonna is strong in the Silath wood once more."

Devis grinned incredulously. "You're seriously telling me I could have done that any time? Why didn't we just do it earlier?" he asked the cleric. Everyone in the cart looked at Zalyn.

"The day this would work wasn't my idea, it was hers," the elf replied. Then the glowing tones of the goddess flowed over Zalyn's voice and added, "But this is only one of the tasks we must see through. Those above are still in peril."

"Hey, goddess lady," Hound-Eye said, pounding a wightling rat into goo, "you think we might get a move on?"

Silently Zalyn waved her hand, and they started rolling slowly down the tunnel.

A booming voice echoed down the passage, shouting out a long string of Elvish curses. The voice was unmistakably Clayn's.

"Oh, no," Mialee whispered, looking up. Soveliss shouted his grandson's name.

"Soveliss?" the voice answered. "Where are you? They toppled me into the shaft. The other two, they're not warriors! Silatham lives, but the man and his wife will never drive back that horde by themselves."

A scream hammered down the shaft, the scream of an elf.

"Darji," Soveliss said to the raven, "can you fly back up the chute?"

The little bird chirped, "Of course!"

"Please find out what you can."

The ranger scowled as another scream fell around their ears. Devis saw Nialma look up for a moment, then the girl resumed her humming, swinging her arms in a dance step that only children know. Darji took off up the cavernous levitation tube.

They picked up speed as the heavy, iron cart rolled down the tracks of the mine tunnel.

The cart bumped across a rough section of track, and they all tumbled into a pile in the rear of the iron box. Mialee pushed Devis off her with a grunt.

"Devis," Mialee said, her aphasia gone at last. "Stay where you are, I'm going to stand on your back."

"Wait, I can just—" Devis began, but Mialee was already climbing off the floor of the accelerating cart.

She nearly fell over backward as the cart picked up speed, but she caught the very lip of the top and heaved herself up to the edge.

A bowshot behind them, a shouting, cursing elf was coming to rest on the ground. Mialee could tell that he was shouting something at the bird fluttering around his head, but the grinding of the iron wheels drowned out the words. Darji spiraled around the elf then flew like a shot back in Mialee's direction.

She heard three grunts of exertion from her left and watched as Soveliss kicked and vaulted up from the floor of the rocking, bounding cart to land on his feet next to her. The man's balance was uncanny.

"Terrible view," Soveliss muttered, then shouted down the tunnel at the man who was his last, tenuous link to the past. "Clayn! Stay there, we'll come back for you!"

Clayn cupped a hand to his mouth to reply, but immediately flung the hand out as a fat, oily rat, which Mialee could see clearly even at this distance, floated down and settled on his shoulder.

"Soveliss! Go! I'll hold them off as long as I can!" the ranger's voice boomed back at them as more and more furry wightling rodents setlled around him.

Mialee gasped involuntarily when she saw wightling elves, groaning and smoldering, float down behind the rats.

Soveliss looked as if he wanted to jump from the cart and run back to aid his imperiled kin. Darji cawed as she reached the cart.

"No, Soveliss! You must go ahead!"

Soveliss threw a salute down the hall.

Clayn, hacking into a pair of descending gray legs, caught the salute and returned it. More and more burning, writhing creatures fell slowly down, and he chopped them all to bits as they came. As the cart rolled on, Mialee saw that many of the squirming pieces were still on fire. Clayn chopped into a vaguely man-shaped mass of flame and one landed atop the stacked kegs of blasting powder.

Fire. Blasting powder.

"Oh, no," Mialee whispered.

<hr />

"And I've got another thing to say, Cava," Favrid said from his shackled, spread-eagled place on the stone wall. "You never did find the secret of the tomb. I did. You're a coward." He laughed bitterly. "The Buried One. That name's too good for you. We should have called you the Incompetent One."

The elf-turned-wight leaped from his rough-hewn deknae throne and hissed into the old man's bruised, bleeding face.

"Don't ever call me by that name, deceiver!" the wight snarled viciously, jabbing his hooked finger into the old man's eye.

Favrid screamed pitiably, and Cavadrec heard something pop. A thin line of green ooze drooled down his chin. He had not tasted his favorite treat in days. He opened one finger and carefully hooked the ruined orb with one razor-sharp claw, expertly severing the optic nerve without damaging the brain. Well, not too much. The old wizard only had to be alive. Nothing in the incantations required an intelligent, or even lucid, sacrifice, only that it must be blood that was spilled on the battlefield of Morkeryth, or the spell would fail.

In a very short time, Favrid's blood would fill the unholy chalice now resting on Cavadrec's trophy shelf. It would blend with a specially prepared mixture of arcane and divine magical components. Cavadrec would drink deeply of the concoction, and the dead would rise at his command.

He had never thirsted so, but timing was crucial. It would happen soon.

He pulled his morsel from the old wizard's eye socket with a pop, and was rewarded with another delectable scream. The wight popped the treat into his mouth and thrust his face in front of the old man's jaw. The empty socket bled profusely, but supernatural senses told Cavadrec his old enemy still had plenty of the stuff left inside him. And he was so hungry. The blood-covered eye was an excellent appetizer for the main course.

Two pinpricks of red light flashed in Cavadrec's empty sockets. He cocked his head to one side like a cat examining an insect it knows cannot escape, and stared into Favrid's remaining eye. The old man stared back, defiantly, but whimpered with agony.

Cavadrec extended the clawed pinky of his left hand and

popped it into the soft jelly. The old fool screamed again. It was dinner music to the wight's wrinkled, pointed ears.

～～～

Mialee landed in Devis's lap.

Her eyes were wide. "Blasting powder! Fire! Duck!" She covered her head, and they all did the same.

Devis felt and heard the boom in equal portions. A searing shock wave struck the back of the cart and pushed it even faster down the tunnel

Mialee pressed her forehead against his chest, but Devis realized she wasn't just looking for a shoulder to cry on. Flaming debris was thundering down the tunnel behind them. He put one arm around Mialee's shoulder and covered his head with his free arm just moments before the flames washed overhead. The heat was incredible, and cinders and small pieces of burning powder rained around them. Devis patted his hair, and Mialee's wild strands, putting out tiny sparks.

A hissing, clattering noise grabbed his attention.

"The treasure!" the bard shouted, a mix of warning and grief.

He pulled Mialee down even further, curling her into a corner and smashing his own body atop hers. He hoped the others were doing the same, because there was no time to do anything else.

Molten metal—the treasure that would never make Devis rich—spattered in softened, ingot-sized chunks all around them. Hound-Eye screamed, and Soveliss snarled in pain. Devis stifled a cry as two thumb-sized points of searing pain struck his back. He wriggled, trying to shake the piece free, but dared not pull off the smoldering vest because it was his only protection. And he was Mialee's only protection. Sizzling metal would pass right through the open latticework of her athelwood armor. Devis dared not move much, even when a third chunk of metal seared into the heel of his boot.

The bard did not have the power to shield them all, but he could ensure that he and Mialee, at least, had a little extra protection. He dragged a tune from his frantic brain and felt the song-spell wrap their bodies in a coat of magical armor. The molten shrapnel on his back and heel stopped sizzling, but the pain of the burns remained. He gritted his teeth and for the first time in his life, said a prayer to Fharlanghn that was completely and utterly sincere.

Cavadrec's lair shook and rumbled. A pair of wolves bounded into the room from one of the many tunnel entrances, howling and stalking the room with obvious and uncharacteristic anxiety. Still, he reminded himself, they were only animals acting on instinct. He decided not to destroy them, but to instead find out what had just set off an earthquake.

"They're coming for you, Cava!" the eyeless, brutalized old man shrieked insanely. Favrid, as near as Cavadrec could see, had been reduced to a screaming lunatic after the wight consumed his eyes. "You can't escape! They won't just bury you! They'll destroy you, Cava!" The old elf began giggling, and it grew into the raving laugh of a madman. "Cava, this fix he's in, because I stole his thirimin," he sang deliriously.

Cavadrec whirled in fury and slashed Favrid's ruined face with splayed claws. He hissed like a cat, longing to tear the old fool into lifeless pieces for daring to bring up their past.

Favrid lifted his battered, bloody head, and the wight heard a gurgle. Blood poured from the old wizard's throat. The impulsive slash had done more damage than Cavadrec intended.

Through bubbling blood, Favrid croaked, "The day of prophecy is at hand, Cava."

Blood flew in a spray from his mouth as he spat the last word, and slumped as his life drained into the cracks in the dusty, stone floor.

"Too soon! Fool!" Cavadrec shouted. Cavadrec leaped to the sacred skull-chalice of Nerull in one bound and had the cup pressed against Favrid's chest with another. As the last of his hated enemy's blood pulsed weakly into the grinning cup, Cavadrec smiled in relief. He felt a dark certainty enter his brain, the hollow, terribly beautiful voice of the god of death. The voice prodded him—not with words, for words were useless to the dead, but with the Reaper's will—to proceed. They had waited long enough.

The liquid in the cup reached the brim. He held the cup to his nose and drank in the sweet aroma of liquid life. Favrid choked one final gasp, then hung limp in his shackles. Cavadrec leered.

With a swirl of ancient robes, the wight moved to his worktable and began adding ingredients to his draught.

Mialee's face pressed into Devis's belly, and she screamed into his leather vest. She could not breathe.

She had to do something. She felt the warmth of a spell suffuse Devis's body and felt vibration in his torso from the quick spell-song he contrived. An armor spell. Fine for them, but she could tell from Hound-Eye's desperate wails that the man was suffering terribly. No doubt the others were, too, they just weren't screaming as loudly as the little thief.

Mialee squirmed in the bard's protective embrace until she faced the orange fire above them, or at least that's what gravity told her.

She wriggled her hands onto her chest and shouted, "I'm sorry!" as she jabbed a fist into Devis's solar plexus.

The bard arched his back, giving Mialee just enough room to maneuver her hands in the motions required by the spell she was casting. Her fingers flew through the precise movements, and she hoped with all her heart that the aphasia potion had truly left her system.

"*Mithral drii!*" she shouted.

The effect was immediate. Mialee felt rather than saw the shield of translucent, silver force materialize directly overhead. It appeared exactly where she'd hoped, far enough away from her to make room for everyone. The shield also cut back the roar of the explosion to a loud rumble.

"Let me up!" she shouted into Devis's belly and was rewarded with a gulp of hot but breathable air when he rolled off her.

Her eyes blinked at the sudden appearance of the wall of flame just overhead. It seemed to be thinning out, and she could tell from the horrible, jouncing ride that they were going much, much faster than the mine cart had been intended to go. The others, in various states of injury but still gratefully alive, huddled under the shield and waited for Hell to cool down, if not freeze over.

They didn't have long to wait. Within half a minute, the ceiling of the tunnel emerged through the grasping flames. Within another half minute, the wind of their passage finally overcame the receding shock wave of the exploding blasting powder.

They bounced along the tunnel. Mialee had no idea how far, measures of distance had never been her strong suit and their dizzying speed made the black rock lining the ancient lava fly by. She flicked the hardened metal chunks from Devis's back with his ridiculous jeweled dagger and heard Hound-Eye whimper as a stoic Nialma gingerly knocked still-hot ingots from the halfling's scorched fur cloak. Zalyn, who bore not a mark, helped Soveliss dig searing bullets from his bare shoulders and armored back. The ranger did not flinch, but hissed frequently. Mialee wondered if the ranger had protected Zalyn as Devis had shielded her, or if hot metal simply wasn't capable of penetrating skin inhabited by a god.

Suddenly the bouncing stopped. Mialee felt the huge iron cart tilt nose down.

They were no longer on the tracks, she realized. They were no longer on anything. The cart was falling.

Cavadrec looked up from his concoction. It was finished. He carried the precious chalice to his shrine and placed the grinning rictus of the skull-cup on a worn altar big enough to hold a half-orc. The surface was black and grimed with centuries of dried sacrifices. Flames rose in the brazier set into the shrine.

The rumbling overhead stopped. He paused and cocked a gray ear toward the ceiling of his lair.

Idiots. The old wizard had thought to intimidate him with the noisy entrance of his supposed saviors. Favrid would never know his folly. That was unfortunate, because his pain would have been a thing of beauty. Cavadrec had known about their "secret" passage for hundreds of years. He also knew the tracks no longer led as far as the fools supposed. He waited a few precious seconds for the satisfying crash. Even if the intruders survived the fall—which he doubted—the rust monster would take care of the rest. It was not his creature in the same sense as the rats, wolves, and other wightlings, but it worked to his advantage in this case all the same.

The lair shook as something terribly heavy came violently to rest in a sea of rusted metal. Cavadrec hissed. Not a thing stood between the wight and total dominion. In a low, quiet voice that soon boomed into a horrible shout, he began the chant that would raise the fallen warriors of Morkeyth.

Devis groaned. His ribs had to be broken, a few of them, anyway. Even so, they'd been extremely lucky. The iron cart had tumbled end-over-end twice, and by sheer, dumb luck, it came to rest on its wheels. From the shrieking thunder of metal grinding on metal that accompanied their landing, he guessed that the sturdy iron box had probably saved their lives.

He blinked and looked around at the others. They were all alive, though Soveliss looked like his arm was broken. Hound-Eye held little Nialma tight, ignoring the bleeding raspberry running the whole length of one muscular, brown arm. Devis blinked when he saw the halfling actually kiss the elf girl's elbow, which she must have skinned. The girl was otherwise unharmed as far as the bard could tell, it looked like Hound-Eye had protected her with his own body. Mialee had a nasty welt on her temple that seeped blood, and her ankle looked twisted in an impossible way. Zalyn the goddess-possessed had her mouth open to little Darji, mouthing the words to a spell.

Devis shook his head. Mouthing? No, she wasn't. They were all talking and making noise, but Devis couldn't hear them. The crash had deafened him.

For the second time in the last ten minutes, Devis prayed silently for Fharlanghn to grant his favorite bard one last favor.

Mialee saw—with some disbelief—Devis shake his head and launch into a panicked, singsong prayer. She could barely hear his words, but it sounded to her as if he was begging for his ears to grow back, or something similar. Yet his softly pointed ears seemed to be one of the few body parts that had escaped injury.

Then she realized that Devis wasn't asking for his ears, but for his hearing. She tried to stand, to assure him the effect had to be temporary—she herself could not hear very well—but pain lanced through her leg and she dropped back to the floor with a yelp.

Her bruised, cut legs stretched straight out in front of her, but the toes of her left foot still pointed at the floor. Blood ringed her ankle, and she could see bits of white bone sticking through the flesh. She winced and bit back a scream. She wouldn't be standing or walking without serious help. Fortunately, she knew just the goddess-filled healer for the job.

"Zalyn," she gasped, "ankle."

The elder elf, looking older and more tired than ever, opened her cupped hands and a little raven flew up, fully healed. Mialee didn't even want to think of what the flames had done to the bird. Darji landed on her shoulder and chirped. Mialee sensed that the line dividing Zalyn and Ehlonna was fading, and it was definitely not Zalyn's impish voice that reached her ears whispering a soft, healing refrain. Mialee's mangled foot turned, toes up. A greenish-gold glow swelled around the bloody wound, then dissipated. The blood was still there, but it had already dried.

She flexed her toes. Not a bit of pain. She thanked Ehlonna/Zalyn wordlessly, and decided not to mention to the goddess that she still hurt everywhere else. She pulled herself to her feet and went to Devis. He pointed to one ear.

"I CAN'T HEAR A THING," the bard said with ridiculous volume. Mialee laughed. Despite his condition he embraced her in relief. They were alive.

After a long time, during which their goddess in cleric's clothing went to each of them in turn to treat their most grievous injuries, including Devis's hearing, Mialee raised her head and looked the bard in the eye. Those eyes grew wide as Mialee placed a hand on either side of his face.

As luck would have it, an earthquake chose that exact moment to strike. Devis lost his balance and they fell to the floor of the cart in a tangle. Their massive vessel gave in to the demands of cruel gravity and tipped onto its side, spilling them all across a field of rusted, jagged metal.

Devis cried out as he felt something pierce his side deeply. All around him, the ocean of rusted metal, corroded beyond belief, roiled like a stormy sea.

Wincing, he pulled himself off the jagged thing that may have once been a long sword and felt blood well inside his vest. The bard pulled a filthy, blackened handkerchief from his pocket in one shaking hand and balled it up. He choked back a wail as he stuffed the cloth ball beneath his vest and into the wound. It might keep him from bleeding to death today only to kill him with an infection in a week.

Mialee! He frantically scanned the area for the elf woman. She'd been about to—

There. She lay on her back, maybe ten feet away. He saw her breast rise and fall. Unconscious, but alive. He looked for the others and found them fanned all around him. All of them but Mialee were moving about, tending to fresh injuries. Zalyn, completely unharmed as usual, floated—floated? Yes, that's exactly what she did, Devis saw—to Hound-Eye, who had gotten the worst of it. His patch was gone and the empty, black socket reminded Devis of the peril they had yet to face. The little halfling still held Nialma tightly to his chest. Hound-Eye had once again put himself between the little girl and harm's way, and this time had truly suffered for it. Two ancient, rusted steel bars were rammed up through his torso on either side of Nialma. Halfling blood streamed down his waist and legs. Somehow Hound-Eye remained conscious and calm. Perhaps, Devis hoped, he couldn't feel it. The halfling had earned that much mercy.

Zalyn/Ehlonna leaned against Soveliss as she shouted more loudly in the din of shrieking metal. Hound-Eye's body rose slowly into the air, the bars grinding out of him. Twin torrents of claret drained from his back onto the rusted surface of the nightmare floor. Nialma, stoic as ever, watched intently as the possessed cleric finished her lengthy incantation and the bleeding trickled to a drip, then stopped completely. Hound-Eye let out a "Wha!" as he spun in mid-air and came to rest gently on his feet. His other wounds still bled, but he would not die today. Not from this particular impalement, anyway.

A low rumbling grew under the groaning metal, and a small, red-brown hillock rose beneath them. Devis felt with dreadful certainty that the cart had not been upset by an earthquake. Something was alive far below them, and it was moving to the surface.

"Run!" he shouted to the others.

"Where?" Hound-Eye yelled over the din.

"That way!" Soveliss shouted, pointing at a distant, narrow opening that Devis could barely see.

The only light in the cavern was coming from the cleric's spells and her eerie, glowing body. The others stumbled toweard the exit, but Devis headed in the exact opposite direction.

Mialee still lay on her back, her only movements the drawing of breath. Scrambling as carefully as he could over the rising tide of jagged-edged metal, Devis reached Mialee just as something huge and brown, with the head of a massive cockroach, burst through the iron shards behind him. Bars and blades and barrel hoops filled the air. Devis ignored the thumping and stabbing pains in his back as he bent over Mialee's form.

She lay unconscious, eyes closed. An ugly bump had risen on her head. Devis's bleeding side made him cry out as he scooped the elf woman into his arms. The cavern reverberated with a keening, screeching explosion of sound unlike anything Devis had ever heard, even in the last few days. The giant, insectoid head reared above the overturned mine cart. With a deafening crash, the creature dived into the metal like a breaching whale. A massive wave rolled toward Devis and Mialee as the creature moved toward them, submerged in the wreckage. The bard faced the wave and saw with relief that Soveliss, Hound-Eye, little Nialma, and the cleric/goddess were nearly to the tiny exit. Devis stumbled across the churning, rusted sea.

"Keep going!" he shouted to the others, though the urging may have been directed as much at himself.

The others were almost out and probably couldn't hear him anyway. Devis knew with grim certainty that he and Mialee were expendable. He had done his part, and Favrid, Ehlonna, and Soveliss would do the rest. Hound-Eye stood at the crack in the stone wall until the last possible second. Then the halfling flipped him a rough imitation of Clayn's ranger salute, turned, and disappeared into the exit.

Devis did the only thing he could think of as the deadly wave rolled closer. He charged as fast as he dared into the massive iron cart, still tipped on its side and only feet away. It was between them and the screaming wake spreading out from the giant insect. He held Mialee close and waited for the end with little hope.

As the wave rolled ever closer, the bard felt wet warmth spread over his hands. He groaned and struggled to see Mialee's face in the dim light from the tunnel far above. She still had not awoken, and now he knew why. The landing had been far worse than he'd realized. Mialee was bleeding to death in Devis's arms.

The bard felt their iron tomb lurch forward with the arrival of the wave. He clutched the dying elf woman to his chest and prepared to go with her.

29

Mialee was jolted awake as she felt her body jerk upward. Her stomach stayed behind, and she choked back bile. Something warm flowed down her chin.

That wasn't bile. That was blood.

Mialee struggled in Devis's grasp, and fire blossomed around the three jagged wounds in her back.

She felt dizzy and weak. Mialee tried to shout, but could only manage a cry as she realized that they were no longer on the relative safety of the tracks. They had fallen, and then ... she could not remember. She summoned the strength to raise one bruised arm and wrap it around the bard's back, and he started, but didn't raise his head.

Mialee's fingertips dug into the leather of Devis's vest with her last ounce of strength as the two of them rode the improbable wave across the cavern.

Devis's heart leaped in his chest. Mialee's fingers pressed against his back. The elf woman lived, but he could feel the blood soaking into his fingerless glove and soaking his forearms.

Acrid, corrosive wind blasted in from the top of the upended cart. They were gradually gaining speed, riding the wave of metal like a sea lion coming to shore. Devis squinted and chanced a glance ahead of them.

The wall of the cavern loomed before his eyes. Just below, he could still see the small crevice through which his friends had escaped. The wave was carrying them straight for it, topside first. If they survived the collision, they should be able to follow the others and the route would be closed behind them by the cart. Devis could not believe his dumb luck, and silently thanked Fharlanghn for hearing his pleas for some good fortune—any good fortune—albeit belatedly.

He folded himself over Mialee's body, pressed the soles of his boots into the "floor" of their ersatz boat, and braced for impact.

The wave was pushing the cart much more slowly than the explosion that blasted them down the tunnel, but the collision was still strong enough to send Devis tumbling head over heels. He slammed back-first and upside down against the stone. Mialee slipped from his grasp. He winced as her head thunked against the iron amid the ringing, alien screams echoing inside the inky blackness. He reached down and slid Mialee awkwardly onto his lap. The girl's breathing came in shallow gasps. She might have minutes, or only seconds.

Think, bard, think! Devis slammed his fist angrily against the iron beneath him.

Fharlanghn's beard, he could be dense sometimes. Mialee had one of the last healing potions in her belt pouch. His fingers searched through the pockets until he found the vial. He pulled her up and dribbled the liquid between her parted lips.

As Devis readjusted Mialee into a more comfortable position, a scroll tube fell from another pouch on Mialee's belt. Zalyn's scroll tube, Devis realized. Better hold on to that. It might still be important, and it would certainly be worth something—"the parchment that saved the world" and all. He tucked the tube into his belt.

The iron cart lurched upward. The gargantuan roach-thing had switched tactics. Devis hoped the big bug wasn't smart enough to realize what would happen if it rolled the cart back onto its wheels.

The bottom few inches of the escape crevice disappeared as the cart jerked upward. The bard heard a faint cough.

"Devis? What—what's happening?"

He couldn't see her face, but he no longer felt fresh warmth spreading over his blood-soaked hands, either. The cart lurched again, and very slowly began listing back from the wall as gravity took charge and tried to right the toppled cart. In the dim glow that broke into their shelter as it fell away from the wall, Devis saw the escape crevice grow more distant with each passing second.

"We're getting out of here," he said, not bothering to ask whether she felt like coming along. "Hold on."

He gripped the elf woman and stood unsteadily, then leaped out into space.

He landed with a jolt that sent fire into his wounded side, but kept his feet. Escape was a few feet away.

"Put me down," Mialee whispered. "I can walk, and you need your arms."

The elf woman slipped gingerly from his grasp and stood briefly on the shifting metal floor before slipping into the crevice. Devis heard her shout in alarm as her feet shot out from under her and she disappeared down the hole. Mialee's voice shrank down into the tunnel and he could not hear her.

As the cart groaned back onto its wheels with a clang, Devis dived into the crevice, landed painfully on his belly, and flew head-first into the darkness.

Clipping down, down the slippery tunnel, he saw the orange glow of firelight flickering at the end of the ride. He did not see Mialee or anyone else.

"Fharlanghn abides," he said, then shouted at the top of his lungs as air that smelled of fetid incense blasted his face. He became delirious from the insane acceleration. "And his favorite bard is comin' to get you, you gray son of a bitch!"

Mialee landed with a hard thump on her backside and tumbled head over heels, coming to rest a few feet from the end of the slippery tunnel. She thought she heard Devis shout something off-color overhead, but could not take her eyes of the scene unfolding before her stunned eyes.

Zalyn . . . no, Ehlonna . . . no, both of them . . . stood before the hideous wight that had killed Mialee, voice booming as she shouted the incantation of the forest goddess that would make the wight vulnerable. The creature ignored the little elf. It had to be him, Mialee realized. It could be no other. The grinning rictus of Cavadrec, the Buried One, turned to regard the new arrival with a flash of red light in its hollow eyes. It extended a horrible, clawed hand toward the wizard girl and crooked a finger to beckon her forward.

"Welcome," Cavadrec hissed. "Would you like to try your luck again?"

Mialee gaped. Aside from Zalyn, her friends were not doing well. Soveliss limped around the wight, the only other person still upright. Hound-Eye and Nialma were huddled in the corner, crying in supernatural terror that had to be the effect of a fear spell. And Favrid . . .

. . . was dead. At least, Mialee hoped he was, because if he lived, his suffering would have been unimaginable. The elf's corpse hung motionless and limp in a pair of rusty, iron shackles embedded in the rough wall. He was covered with blood, cuts, gashes, and bruises. He had endured grievous torture. Where his gentle, laughing eyes had once twinkled with mischief, there were only empty, bloody sockets. His throat was torn open as if by some kind of animal.

Mialee placed a hand to her mouth and choked back bile. No, she thought, not an animal, but Cavadrec. And with Favrid dead, all was lost.

The elf woman drew in a quick breath of fetid, foul air and felt for the scroll pouch. There was still one wizard here, and she had to try casting the spell. She kept her eyes on Cavadrec as she frantically patted her belt pouches. Where was the blasted thing?

The wight lost interest when she didn't rise to its challenge, and turned to block a long sword blow from Soveliss with the black, skull-topped staff.

The scroll was gone. Mialee felt sick. She collapsed, dropped her head between her knees, and pressed her palms against her temples. Everyone was doomed.

"Coming *throoooooooooooough*!" echoed a familiar voice down the tunnel, and Devis slammed into Mialee head-first. They rolled into a tangle of arms and legs behind the bellowing Zalyn-goddess.

Cavadrec laughed as the pair struggled to disentangle themselves and stand.

"How very romantic," he cackled. "Linelle, what have you been teaching these children?"

Linelle? Mialee blinked, and then realized he was talking to Zalyn. Linelle must have been her name when Cava was alive.

Behind the wight, Mialee saw Soveliss creep forward and raise the Mor-Hakar. Without looking, Cavadrec twirled his black staff and slammed the end into Soveliss's gut. The elf grasped his belly with an "oof!" and dropped to his knees. His long sword clattered to the ground, and the hand holding the Mor-Hakar slapped against the floor as Soveliss caught himself from toppling forward. The ranger's open palm pressed the hilt of the short sword into the stone while he clutched at his abdomen with the other, struggling to draw breath.

Mialee and Devis helped each other stand. Mialee felt the wetness on the bard's right side and realized he was bleeding badly. She fumbled for her last potion and failed to find that, either.

She licked her lips and knew where the potion had gone. "Devis, you idiot," she whispered urgently as Zalyn and Cavadrec squared off. "Why didn't you take the potion yourself? You're going to bleed to death!"

The elf woman felt the bard lean against her, and his face was pale and bloodless.

"You first," Devis said deliriously and showed her his blood-soaked hands. "Couldn't lose . . . *yrrrrr*," he managed.

The bard's eyes rolled back and he dropped heavily against her, unconscious. She lowered him gently to the floor and pulled his head into her lap as green-gold energy started filling the room with a warm glow. The shrine of the death god, smoldering with Cavadrec's interrupted invocation, blazed higher in the rush of oxygen and fresh air that the swelling power of the forest god provided.

The brazier on the terrible shrine of Nerull flared and went dark. A grinning goblet made from an ancient, elf skull stared back at Mialee. She felt a surge as the goddess that walked as a cleric finished her invocation, severing the wight's connection to Nerull. The wight screamed and staggered, thrown off balance. Now, if the arcane scroll were read, it would be over. She watched Soveliss cough up black, bloody phlegm, struggling to his feet with the Mor-Hakar gripped in one gloved fist and blind hatred flashing in his eyes.

If they could just read the scroll, the wight would be vulnerable, or as close as they could hope to make it. Mialee would accept the risk in a heartbeat. If only she hadn't somehow lost the precious scroll tube. She wrapped her arms around Devis, propped up but unconscious, and sighed miserably.

A loud crack resounded in the chamber. Cavadrec brought the heavy end of his black staff across Ehlonna/Zalyn's jaw and sent her little body flying through the air. Mialee saw the elder of Silatham, and with her, the Mother of Elves, slam with a sickening crunch into the stone, then fall chillingly still.

With dreadful certainty, Mialee saw that the goddess-cleric had been fooled by a very simple deception. The staff that bore the icon of the god of death was not at all an unholy tool of the Reaper. The black staff was a powerful magic weapon infused with arcane energy. "A wand disguised as a prayer book" was how wizards and sorcerers described such deceptive artifacts.

Mialee cried out involuntarily as the staff cracked again, knocking Soveliss back, but the nimble ranger stayed on his feet, the Mor-Hakar a menacing sliver in his hand.

Mialee buried her face in Devis's hair and gazed down his body. Too bad, she thought madly, so much will be lost.

Her eyes fell on the ornately engraved tube tucked into an open pouch on the bard's belt. The scroll! She reached forward, yanked out the tube and leaped to her feet. She heard Devis's head thunk against the stone and he barked a cry of pain as he was jolted awake. He'd thank her later, if they were still alive. She thumbed the stopper off the end of the scroll tube and unrolled the yellowed parchment.

Mialee heard another crack and a pair of thumps, and saw Soveliss on his knees. He still held the Mor-Hakar. She frantically read over the lengthy scroll—damn Favrid's wordiness!—as the wight stepped toward the staggered ranger. Cavadrec raised the ebony staff like a club, preparing to deliver a blow that would crush Soveliss's skull.

Mialee began reciting the words on the scroll.

Devis leaped in front of her with a mad yell, driven by some reserve of strength she could hardly believe remained in his nearly bloodless body. She continued reading aloud and felt the sparkle of magic surround her and fill the air.

As she continued reading, her gentle voice rose to a hoarse shout.

She thought Devis was moving to help Soveliss, but to her shock, the bard ran right past the ranger and grasped the grinning goblet set before the extinguished shrine of Nerull. His hand curled with smoke. Mialee smelled burning leather and flesh. The chalice must be anathema to anything that was not soiled by the Reaper's foul touch. Despite what must have been terrible pain, the bard raised the chalice in the air and turned.

"Hey, Bright Eyes!" he bellowed madly. "You can kill the ranger or save your cocktail. What'll it be?"

Devis tipped the skull-cup, and a drop of something thick and red dripped to the floor, where it sizzled as it touched the stone.

The wight froze, then turned slowly to regard the ranger. "I choose both," Cavadrec snarled, holding his staff in one hand and reaching out with the other.

Mialee saw the glow of a spell stretch from the wight's talons and wrap around the chalice. Devis grasped the cup with both hands and struggled against the pull of Cavadrec's magic grip, but only skidded across the floor on the heels of his boots.

Mialee finished reading the scroll. A blast of blue lightning exploded from the paper's surface. She clutched the parchment with white knuckles and absorbed the barrage with her eyes squeezed shut. She was reasonably certain this wasn't one of the spell's intended effects. She must have mispronounced something, perhaps a single word. As blue energy crackled painfully from nerve to nerve throughout her body, she forced her eyes open to see what, if anything, she had wrought. The magic arcing through her body made everything appear to move as if in syrup.

The chalice tumbled end over end, splattering blackish-red gore all over Devis, who was whirling his arms in a hopeless attempt to keep from tumbling over backward. He dropped hard onto his backside with a shout of pain.

Cavadrec screamed and crouched to pounce for the precious artifact. The ranger was forgotten. The ebony staff no longer gleamed with black light, but was only a simple shaft of gnarled wood. The wight hissed and dropped the staff, brandishing hooked claws. He swiped the air in a screaming rage, forcing Soveliss back. Finally, the wight landed a blow on the ranger, who slammed against the temple wall, staggering and dazed.

Cavadrec loomed over the ranger. He backhanded the man across the jaw, knocking Soveliss's head against the wall, but somehow the elf avoided the next blow and slipped away sideways. The wight would be back on him in seconds.

Aside from the disenchanted staff, Mialee could see little evidence that the scroll had worked. The wight still seethed with his own, innate power. Soveliss would be ripped limb from limb.

Mialee had played Favrid's part with little apparent success. Soveliss was down and at the wight's mercy. Favrid was dead. Zalyn was unconscious, possibly dead. Devis was dying, Hound-Eye was paralyzed. She'd have to try her own scheme. Maybe the wight couldn't hit what it couldn't see. The spell was untried, but she would never get another chance.

Mialee waved a series of precise hand motions in the air and whispered, "*Nehdarn*, Soveliss."

The ranger disappeared. The invisibility spell had come in handy after all.

Cavadrec slashed the empty air in fury, then turned to an enemy he could see: Devis. The bard was still struggling to regain his feet. Cavadrec slapped Devis across the face with the back of a bony fist, driving him down to the floor with a thud where the man lay still. The wight whirled toward Mialee, red eyes flashing, and took one long step toward the fallen elf woman.

"For Silatham!" Soveliss shouted from the empty air.

A crack, then a crevice, then a crater split Cavadrec's forehead between the eyes as the ranger hammered the invisible blade of the Mor-Hakar through the creature's skull. The point erupted from the back of the wight's head in a spray of bone and gray matter. A deafening wail erupted from the creature that had once been Cava, cleric of Ehlonna. The wight writhed like a pinned insect around the blade, which gradually became visible but stayed fast. The unearthly howl filled the lair.

Finally, Cavadrec's screech settled into a hiss of fetid air. His body, instantly rigid, toppled backward onto the cold, stone floor.

"For Elyrra," a quiet voice said.

Soveliss, now almost completely visible, bent over the corpse and gave the short sword a brutal twist. The wight's head cracked open, releasing a fountain of matter. The ruined skull lolled over to face Mialee. Two red lights in the pits of the hideously empty sockets flickered once, twice, then died with a curl of acrid smoke. Cavadrec's flame was extinguished.

The ranger wiped gore from the Mor-Hakar onto the wight's torn robe. For the first time since Mialee laid eyes on the man, he looked at peace.

A long minute passed. Devis tried to stand, then resorted to dragging himself toward Mialee, who sat dumbfounded on the floor. As he struggled to reach her, she gazed mutely around the lair. Hound-Eye and little Nialma were walking toward her in a daze, both speechless. Her eyes passed over Favrid—the elf's fate was still too fresh and horrible for her to look at him. Soveliss stood over the gray corpse, already slowly rotting away. Finally, her gaze fell on Zalyn.

The rose blossom of scarlet on the wall above her, and the wet trail leading down behind her to the floor, told Mialee all she needed to know. The elder's body, at least, showed no sign of the wightling disease. She was simply dead. Zalyn had left with Ehlonna to join Favrid. Darji, mute and mundane bird though she now was, perched on Zalyn's tiny boots. It cocked its eye at Mialee, then spread its wings and disappeared down one of the many cave entrances dotting the lair. A single caw echoed back to her.

Mialee smelled burning hair and frantically patted her locks to extinguish a few persistent blue flames. She felt the back of her hand slap flesh and Devis said, "Hey!"

"Sorry. On fire. Now I'm out."

Devis's arm slipped around her shoulders and she leaned into him with a weary sigh, careful not to aggravate his injuries further. Devis winced, but pressed a fist into the hole in his side. He grinned weakly at Mialee, and she saw some color had returned to his face. "The bleeding's slowed down," he croaked. Either that, or I'm running out. You?"

"Just a little singed," she whispered.

The lair lurched and the floor tilted, sending them all sprawling in the direction of the caves leading out to the lava tubes. A great rumbling shook everything in sight.

The wight was dead, his spell disrupted, but apparently the god of death had decided to cheat. Or maybe Cavadrec had somehow kept the dead mountain in check for a thousand years. Whatever the reason, sleeping Morsilath was waking up.

Hound-Eye howled in pain. A thin jet of magma blasted him in the toe. Mialee saw it was just a herald of much worse to come as cracks appeared in the stone all around and the air filled with fire.

Cavadrec's throne lurched from its resting place and began to slice toward them.

Darji flapped back into the chamber and then disappeared up another lava tube.

The throne slid toward them, front end first, chipping rock shards from the floor and launching them in a shower ahead of itself. Orange lava flashed through widening cracks behind it. Devis remembered how the iron cart protected them from the thing in the metal pile and had a terrible idea. The throne might block the flow of lava down their escape tunnel long enough for them to get away—if they could find a tunnel that really led to the surface and not back into a wall of magma.

The bard got behind the sliding throne and shoved hard with his shoulder, guiding it toward the tunnel entrance Darji had selected. Soveliss saw what he was up to and he and Mialee joined in. The trio pushed, shouted, and cajoled the massive deknae artifact into place a foot or so in front of their intended exit. Hound-Eye and Nialma were already heading up the tube. Soveliss dashed after them.

"After you!" Devis screamed at the top of his lungs, gesturing for Mialee to step in.

"You first!" Mialee shouted.

The bard gripped Mialee by the arm and half-pushed, half-pulled her into the opening, then squeezed in behind. Hound-Eye, Nialma, and Soveliss were twenty feet ahead. Mialee and Devis stumbled up the steep, smooth, shaking walls of the escape route.

The eruption of Morsilath finally broke into Cavadrec's lair. The group had moved only a few yards up the tube when Mialee felt heat at her back and the tube filled with blazing orange light. She looked back and saw their improvised shield heat up from black to red to orange, then it was gone.

The inferno crawled up the tunnel after them.

Mialee thought furiously. If only she hadn't used the shield the last time something was going to fry them.

The pearl.

She had forgotten it since the incident at the tavern. She reached into her pouch. It was still there, thank Ehlonna. She pinched it in two fingers, running all the while and trying to recall the incantation that would place the shield at their backs.

The round, invisible force wall snapped into existence behind her. The spell was just wide enough to fit in this tube. If she could pull it behind them and adjust its edges just right, she might be able to hold back the lava long enough for them to reach the surface. Mialee steeled her mind to push back against it when the lava struck. The lava itself would provide the propulsion.

Despite her concentration, the shield spell slammed into her back when the rising lava smashed into it. The party was pressed backward in a pile against the shield effect. Mialee screamed from the unbearable heat, but the force wall held. Despite the pain, she spread her arms and legs wider, pressing against the clutch of bodies—if one of her friends slipped past her, they would slide through the shield and be incinerated.

The pressure forced them up the tube fast enough to make Mialee's eyes water and her ears hurt. She struggled to keep the disc of force pressed against the molten rock at right angles to the smooth walls of the tube. Bits of rock were shaved off by the magical edges of the disk and covered them like charcoal powder. She worried about how long the tunnel was. Would the spell last all the way to the top?

Mialee squinted against the wind and flakes of stone. She risked looking ahead for a split second, trusting the shield spell to her subconscious control.

Several yards ahead, a white-yellow light, roughly circular, awaited her. Seconds later, the five of them blasted out into the open air. Mialee gaped as the party rode the spell up, up, up, and then down, down, down into the forest, where Ehlonna's personal protection kept the molten stone from burning her children.

"Gods," Mialee whispered, "it's beautiful."

Her concentration broke. The shield spell fizzed and died. Gravity and entropy pulled the five apart only a few feet before they crashed into the boughs of an enormous old Silath tree.

With a chorus of cracked wood, barked curses, and terrified screams, they dropped gradually through the tree to the ground.

Mialee marveled. They'd landed smack in the middle of Silatham. The undead were dead, and the elven village was alive.

Epilogue . . . Mialee smiled over her glass of milk at the last remaining family in Silatham. She raised her glass to Pell's warm grin when he caught her glance. Ehlonna's newest cleric—and the reason the lot of them weren't all still lying on the ground covered with burns—clasped Zalyn's golden holy symbol and nodded, mouthing *thank you*. Delia and Hound-Eye played a game of hide-and-seek with little Nialma, who they all knew was under the bed in the next room. Still the halfling loudly professed that rat-girl had just disappeared. That drew excited giggles from beneath the bed, and the sound rang like music through the cozy home. The living village had saved Nialma's parents from the fire. Now, it seemed, the family might be about to grow by one growling halfling.

Mialee leaned back in her chair and stretched, yawning and considering. The music, and Ehlonna herself, had kept the mountain in check. Morsilath stewed, rumbling now and then, but had not covered the land with lava.

"Of all the damn-fool luck," Devis had said when they'd dropped with a thud amid the zombie carnage.

Silatham's survival was miraculous, but the cost to its population had been dear. Thousands now lay rotting outside, gray meat-things covered with flies. They'd cleared this house—Pell and Delia's—of the foul things, but the village needed time to rest. A long cleanup job lay ahead for the last ranger of Silatham. Favrid and Zalyn were gone, but Soveliss had sworn on the Mor-Hakar he would see the place filled again with life within his years.

"And who knows, I might reach two-thousand yet," the elf said after taking his oath.

"Check this out," Devis said, scooting into the chair next to Mialee's at the table. "Pell had a bottle of very, very old dwarf whiskey. I saw a man get killed over a bottle of this stuff in Dogmar. It's incredible."

He smacked the bottle on the table in front of her and placed a pair of shot glasses on either side.

"I have milk."

"Mialee, we just saved the world. Have a drink with me."

Mialee pushed her milk aside and grinned at the bard.

"One drink?" he asked.

"One drink," she said.